A DIGIT OF THE MOON

A DIGIT OF THE MOON

A HINDOO LOVE STORY

TRANSLATED FROM
THE ORIGINAL MS.

F. W. BAIN

GYAN

Published by

Gyan Publishing House
5, Ansari Road
Daryaganj, New Delhi-110002
Phone: 011-47034999, 9811692060
E-mail: books@gyanbooks.com

Distribution Network
gyanbooks.com
India, USA, Canada, UK, Australia

ISBN: 978-93-7414-390-2 (PB)

First Published, 1910

2nd Impression 2025

Printed at: Gyan Press, Delhi.

A DIGIT OF THE MOON
Author: F. W. BAIN

A
DIGIT OF THE MOON.

मथितार्णववीचिविलासिनि
नरवंशप्रिये
गगणाद्वतीर्यसुधानिधि
जगद्न्धमध्ये
त्रिजगन्ति नुमः स्तनमण्डलम्
धृतशक्तित्रयम्
प्रलयस्थितिसर्गपयोधरम्
शयनम् शरणम्

A DIGIT OF THE MOON

(बालातपरक्ताशशिनी)

A HINDOO LOVE STORY

TRANSLATED FROM THE ORIGINAL MS.

BY

F. W. BAIN

SEVENTH EDITION

METHUEN & CO. LTD.
ESSEX STREET, LONDON, W.C.
OXFORD: PARKER & SON

TO

MY WIFE.

PREFATORY NOTE TO SECOND EDITION.

THE better to illustrate how, in Hindoo mythology, the ideas of *a beautiful woman, the Moon, and the Sea,* dissolve and disappear into one another, I have placed on the fly-leaf of this edition a single stanza, drawn from another part of my MS., which characteristically exemplifies that *dissolving view:* subjoining here, for the benefit of the uninitiated, a literal translation:

O thou lovely Incarnation of the Nectar-dropping Moon, come down from Heaven to lighten our Darkness: Delight of the Race of Man: retaining in thy Womanhood the dancing Play of the Waves of that Sea of Milk out of which thou wert originally churned by the Gods: we the Three Worlds (i.e. of Childhood, Manhood, and Age) do worship the Orb of thy Bosom that possesses for us a Threefold Mystical Feminine Energy[a]*: being a Pitcher of Milk for us, when we are Born:*

[a] The last lines contain recondite philosophical allusions to the Creation, Preservation, and Destruction of the World, and other matters, in technical terms which defy translation. Life in Hindoo philosophy, as in that of the Middle Ages, carries about with it a perfume of death: there is in its atmosphere something melancholy, and even a little morbid, like the slow tolling of a bell.

a Pillow for us, in the Middle of the Path of Life: and a Shrine, in which we take refuge to die at the last.

But we lose, in a literal prose version, the reverberation, and the echo of the Sea, which undertones the meaning of the words like the accompaniment to a song. This *sound* we might make some attempt to preserve, without doing violence to the *sense*, as follows;

Like a New Moon's exquisite Incarnation,
    In the Ebb and Flow of a Surging Sea,
Wave-breasted Beauty, the whole Creation
    Wanes, and waxes, and rocks on thee!
For we rise and fall on thy Bosom's Billow
    Whose heaving Swell is our Home Divine,
Our Chalice at Dawn, and our hot Noon's Pillow,
                    Our Evening's Shrine.

Woolacombe Bay, April 29, 1901.

PREFACE TO FIRST EDITION.

A DIGIT OF THE MOON is the sixteenth part of a much longer work, entitled *The Churning of the Ocean of Time*[a]. A well-known Hindoo legend recounts how the gods and antigods assembled to churn the ocean of milk[b] for the nectar of immortality. After throwing in herbs of various kinds, they churned it with Mount Mandara, and obtained the nectar, with certain other things, one of which was the MOON, who by the way is often called 'the Lord of Herbs.'

But in Sanskrit, the Moon, like the Sun, is a male. Hindoo poets get over this difficulty, when they want a female Moon, by personifying his attributes, or making a part do duty for the whole. Thus, his disc is divided into sixteen parts, called '*streaks*' or '*digits*,' and a beautiful woman is '*a digit of the moon*.'

[a] *Sańsára-ságara-manthanam.*

[b] For *milk* the author has substituted a technical word which means *the world considered as the scene of never-ending transmigrations.* ('*O world! O life! O time!*') By this he implies that the *nectar* of his work is the residuum of much churning of life and experience of the world, and that it is destined to be immortal.

The whole work, then, called '*The Churning of the Ocean of Time*,' is, like the Moon, divided into sixteen parts, each named after one of the digits of the Moon. The one now before the reader is called *A Digit of the Moon, turned red by the rays of the dawning Sun*[c]. The point lies in the play on the word *red*, which in the original also means '*enamoured*,' '*in love*.' That is to say, that the heroine of the story 'turns red,' *i.e.* falls in love with the hero, whose name, it will be found, is Súryakánta, or 'Sunstone.'

I little thought, ten years ago, that it would ever be my lot to play, as it were, the part of Boccaccio, and bring forth meat from the eater, stories from a plague. Yet here also the unexpected came about, in the following way.

Considering how recently Europe has become aware of the very existence of a Sanskrit literature, I had often wondered whether there might not be hidden away, here and there, in the vast ocean of India, literary treasures still undiscovered, which future 'churning' might bring

[c] I have never experienced a stranger or more delightful sensation than when, as I was translating this work, I saw this very phenomenon on the Ghauts at Mahábaleshwar: a blood-red Moon going down into the hills at early dawn, with the Sun rising on the opposite peaks. Only the redness which the poet ascribes to the Sun was of course due to the haze of the atmosphere.

up. But I did not expect that my question would ever receive a practical answer. However, a few years ago, when the plague was decimating the city of Poona, carrying off its victims by hundreds a day, personal acquaintance with some of the officers appointed by Government to cope with the enemy put it into my power to do a slight service to an old Marátha Brahman, whose name, by his own particular desire, I suppress. My 'service' was indeed a mere trifle, a thing of which no Englishman would have thought twice. Hindoos, however, look on these matters with very different eyes. An Englishman's house may be his castle, but a Hindoo's house is a shrine, a holy of holies, which for unhallowed footsteps to invade is desecration. I was amused to find that my old Brahman regarded me almost as though I had preserved his family from nameless and everlasting infamy. And when he subsequently discovered that I was a humble student of the 'polished, sacred' language, and could make shift to admire his beloved Kálidás in the original, his esteem for me rose to a degree almost embarrassing. He came two or three times to see me, and took an obvious pleasure in dilating on the beauties of his ancient authors to one who was at least a good listener. But it struck me as curious, that every time he went away he seemed as it were labouring to deliver himself of some important communication, which nevertheless he shrank from discovering to me; and he always eventually departed, with an air of some confusion, and his secret left untold. I thought at the time that he was only nerving himself to make some request of me, of which he doubted the reception, and was unable to screw his courage to the sticking-point. But I was mistaken.

Our interviews came to an abrupt conclusion. The plague stepped in and swept his family clean away, carrying off his wife, all his children, and various others of his kin, leaving him alone untouched—but not for long. One evening, when I came home late, having been out nearly all day, I found on my doorstep a messenger who had been waiting for me, with the inexhaustible patience of an Oriental, for many hours. The plague had remembered my old Brahman at last, and he had sent to ask me to come and see him, 'on business of importance.' I went off accordingly to a segregation camp, whither he had been removed, and, much to my relief, arrived in time to find him conscious: for he was a fine old gentleman, and when a Brahman is a gentleman, he is a striking type of humanity. He confused me by thanking me, for the hundredth time, for my good offices, adding, however, that they had been, in a certain sense, wasted, as he was the only one left of his family, and now he also, he was glad to say, was going the same way. He said, that he had been anxious to see me before he died, because he had something of value to give me. Hereupon he produced what the uninitiated might have taken for a packet of ladies' long six-button gloves, pressed together between two strips of wood about the size of a cheroot box, and tied round with string; but which from experience I knew to be a manuscript [d]. He handed it to me, observing that it had been in the possession of his family from a time beyond memory, and that nothing would ever have induced him to part with it, had any of that family remained to possess it ; but as they were all gone, and as, moreover, it would certainly be burned by the plague authorities as soon as he was dead, it was mine, if I cared to accept it. If not, he said, with an effort to smile, no matter : it could, like a faithful wife, enter the fire on the death of its owner : yet that would be a pity, for it was worth preserving. I accepted his present, and he bade me farewell. I took leave of the old man, not without emotion, for grief and approaching death had converted his face to the very incarnation of misery ; and I learned on enquiry that he died, about thirty-six hours afterwards, in the early morning.

Notwithstanding the hints let fall by its former owner, I own I was dubious as to the value of my MS., for Hindoos will admire anything in Sanskrit. But when—after having redeemed it with difficulty from the ordeal of fire and the plague authorities by subjecting it to severe fumigations—I fell to examining it [e], I apologised

[d] Though I make no attempt to assign a date to this MS., the reader should observe that in India printing has not superseded hand work. The Hindoos have religious prejudices against printed books, and they will not use them in their temples, or for sacred purposes.

[e] A well written MS. in the *Déwanágari* character, is hardly, if at all, inferior to print.

to the *manes* of my old Brahman for doubting his judgment, and blessed him for his present, which is, I will venture to say, unique in literature. But I will leave the reader to judge of it for himself[f], warning him only that no language loses so much by translation as the Sanskrit; and advising him, for his own sake, to read it consecutively through, or he will lose much[g]. I cannot refrain from observing, however, that it differs from the general run of classical Sanskrit productions in two very striking particulars—the simplicity of its style, and the originality of its matter. As to the last, every body knows that classical Sanskrit authors have no originality. They do but rhetorically reset and embellish notorious themes: such originality as they exhibit lying, not in their subject, but its treatment. Our author is an exception. Whoever he was, he must have possessed the gift of imagination: for though the plan of the story was doutless suggested by the *Wétála-panchawimshatiká*, yet so novel and poetical is the use made of it that it may fairly claim to owe but little to its source, while all the particular stories are curious and original. The book differs, again, in a remarkable manner from other classical products of the Hindoo Muse in the simplicity of its style. The author would seem to have deliberately chosen the epic[h] rather

[f] At some future time I hope to translate the remainder, or part of it.

[g] Its principal beauty lies in the skill of its climax, which is lost by neglecting the order.

[h] The poem is written in *shlókas*, or *anushtubh*, with oc-

than the classic style as his model. We find here none of that artificiality, that straining and effort at style for its own sake, that perverse elaboration, those insipid intolerable *shléshas* and interminable compounds which reach a climax in the appalling concatenations of e.g. the *Kádambarí*. Mature Hindoo literature exhibits precisely the same tendency as its architecture: ornament is piled on ornament with aimless, tasteless extravagance, till the whole becomes nauseous, and all unity is smothered and annihilated under a load of rhetorical gewgaws. Just as the rank and luxuriant growth of a creeper will sometimes drain of its juices, dry up, and destroy the tree it was designed to adorn, so the over devolopment of gaudy rhetorical blossoms and effeminate literary prettinesses has desiccated and broken the spring of the Hindoo mind. The best things in the literature are just those which are simplest, and therefore as a rule oldest. Literary arabesque nearly always indicates and springs from the absence of anything to say; a poverty of creative ideas. But our author has really a story to tell, and can therefore afford to exhibit it in naked unadorned simplicity.

Finally, the words which stand as a motto on the title-page have a history of their own. They are the closing lines of the *Shakuntalá*, and they mean, briefly: *O Shiwa, grant that I may never be born again.* There is a *curiosa*

casional deviations (as e.g. the conclusion) into more elaborate metres.

felicitas in their application to the conclusion of the story, where indeed I found them, scribbled in the margin by another hand; and though it cannot be proved, I am convinced that they were placed there by my old Brahman himself (who had Kálidás by heart), when he took his farewell of the MS., in an access of grief and despair at feeling his family annihilated and himself deprived of all that had made his life worth living, by the plague. Let us hope that the old man has had his wish, and that '*the purple-tinted god*' has '*destroyed his rebirth.*'

Mahábaleshwar, 1898.

CONTENTS.

[For the convenience of the English reader I have drawn up this table. The original contains none.]

Note.—The Vignette is a rude sketch by the translator from an old bust of Ganésha. He has only one tusk, and should have four arms, but they have got broken. His favourite vehicle is a mouse or rat, and his trunk is always considered to be smeared with vermilion. He is the God of Success, and the Remover of Obstacles, and woe to the man who should neglect to conciliate him, at the opening of any undertaking!

A DIGIT OF THE MOON.

A Digit of the Moon.

INTRODUCTION.

INVOCATION [a].

May the kindly three-eyed god [b], *who stained his throat deep-purple by the draught of deadly poison which he swallowed for the preservation of the world, preserve you. May the Elephant-faced One* [c] *sweep away with his trunk all impediments to my thoughts, and may Wání* [d] *inspire into my mind for every thought its proper word.*

THERE lived formerly, in a certain country, a king, called Súryakánta [e]. And his armies, guided

[a] Some such benedictory exordium as this is regarded as indispensable by every Sanskrit author: yet it is remarkable that Kálidás is careless of the rule; *e.g.* his *Cloud* and his *Seasons* begin at once without any invocation at all.

[b] Shiwa. [c] Ganésha or Ganapati. See Day I.

[d] Saraswatí, the goddess of speech.

[e] *i.e.* 'sun-beloved;' the name of a fabulous gem 'sunstone' (cp. 'moonstone'), said to possess magical properties and exhibit them when acted upon by the rays of the sun.

by Valour and Policy, had penetrated in all directions to the shore of the ocean, and his intellect had gone to the further shore of all the sciences, so that one thing only was unknown to him, woman, and the love of woman. He was, as it were, the very incarnation of the spirit of misogyny, beautiful exceedingly himself, to scorch with the hot rays of his glory the despairing hearts of all fair women who might chance to cast eyes upon him, yet himself cold as snow to their own melting glances. And as time went on, his ministers became full of concern for the future of the kingdom, for they said: The King has no son, and if he should die, everything will go to ruin for want of an heir. So they took counsel among themselves, and sending for them wherever they could find them, they threw in his way temptations in the form of beautiful women, raining on him as it were showers of the quintessence of all the female beauty in the world. But all was of no avail: for no matter what shape it took, the celestial loveliness of those ladies made no more impression on the King's mind than a forest leaf falling on the back of a wild elephant. Then the ministers fell into despair, exclaiming: Truly there is a point at which virtues become vices. It is well for a King to avoid the wiles of women; but out on this woman-hating king! the kingdom will be undone for him. And they took counsel again among themselves, and made representations to the King, exhorting him to marriage. But he would not listen to anything they could say. So being at their wits' end, they caused it to be bruited about without the King's knowledge, by means of their spies, that they would give a crore[f] of gold pieces to any one who could produce a change in the mind of the King, and inspire him with an inclination for marriage. But though many charlatans presented themselves and performed incantations and other such devices, no one could be found able to effect the desired end. On the contrary, the King's hostility to the other sex increased so much, that he punished every woman who came within the range of his sight by banishing her from the kingdom. And in their fear lest the kingdom should be wholly deprived of its women, the ministers had to place spies about the King, who ran before him wherever he went, and made all the women keep out of his way. And this task was as difficult as standing on the edge of a sword, for all the women in the kingdom were drawn to

[f] Ten millions.

see him by love and curiosity as if he were a magnet[g] and they so many pieces of iron.

Then one day there came to the capital a certain painter[h]. And he, as soon as he arrived, made enquiries as to the wonders of that city. Then the people told him: The greatest wonder in our city is our King, Súryakánta, himself. For though he is a king, nothing will induce him to have anything to do with women, from the peacock of whose beauty he flies as if he were a snake. And yet he is himself like a second god of love, so that here is the marvel: that one whom the Fish-bannered god[i] has created as a sixth weapon to cleave the hearts of the female sex should have no curiosity to exert his power. Should the sun refuse to warm, or the wind to blow? But when the painter heard this he laughed, and said: I possess a charm that would act like the sun upon its gem[k]. And one of the spies of the ministers heard him, and went and told them of his arrival and his brag.

g A kind of play on the King's name: *Lóhakánta* means a loadstone.

h This method of bringing lovers together is part of a Hindoo story-teller's romantic machinery.

i The Hindoo Cupid, who is said to possess five bewildering weapons.

k Alluding to the King's name: see n. p. 1.

And they immediately summoned that painter and questioned him, telling him the whole state of the case, and promising him the reward if he could make his words good. And the painter said : Contrive that the King shall send for me, and leave the rest to me.

So the ministers went and told the King : Sire, there has arrived in your capital a painter, whose equal in skill is not to be found in the three worlds. And when the King heard it he was delighted, for he was himself skilled in the art of painting and all other arts ; and he caused the painter to be brought into his presence. But he, when he came, was amazed at the extraordinary beauty of the King, and he exclaimed : O King, you have caused me to obtain the fruit of my birth in bestowing on me the priceless boon of a sight of your incomparable beauty. And now only one more thing remains. I implore your Majesty to let me make a copy of it, in order that in future I may never be without it. For the sun warms even when reflected in a poor mirror. Then the King said : Show me first specimens of your skill. But beware that you show me no women, otherwise it will be worse for you. So the painter showed him a collection of pictures of all the countries in the world, but among them he had secretly placed the portrait of a woman. And as the King was turning over the pictures, one by one, he suddenly came upon that portrait. But the moment he looked at it, he fell to the ground in a swoon.

Then the painter laughed, and said to the ministers: The cure is effected: pay the physician his fee. But they replied: We must first be sure that the patient is really cured. The painter replied: You will soon find that out. Look to the King, and restore him, and see what he says when he comes to himself and finds that I am not here. For in the meanwhile I will go out of the room.

Then the ministers summoned attendants, who fanned the King with palm-leaves, and sprinkled him with water scented with sandal. And the King revived, and instantly looking round, exclaimed: The painter, the painter! The ministers said: Sire, he is gone. But when the King heard that, he changed colour, and his voice trembled, and he said: If you have allowed him to escape, I will have you all trampled to death by elephants before the sun goes down. So they went out quickly and found the painter, and fetched him in again before the King. And he fell at the King's feet, saying: May the King forgive me! Alas! my evil fortune must have mixed up that lady's portrait among my other pictures, to bring me to destruction. But the King said: O most admirable of all painters, past, present, or to come, know that you have conferred a benefit upon me by exhibiting that portrait to me, which I could not repay even with my whole kingdom. And beyond doubt, that lady must have been my wife in a previous existence, for emotions such as these point unmistakeably to a former life. Now then, tell me, of what land is her father the king? For certain I am, that it is a portrait, for such beauty as hers could not have been conceived by any mortal brain. None but the Creator himself could have fashioned her. Then the painter smiled, and said: O King, be warned by me. Dismiss this lady from your mind, and think of her no more; otherwise my carelessness may turn out to have been the cause of your ruin. But the King said: Painter, no more. Choose, either to tell me who she is, and be loaded with gold; or not; and I will load you with chains, and imprison you in a loathsome dungeon, with neither food nor water, till you do.

Then the painter said: King, since there is no help for it, and your fate will have it so, learn, that this is the portrait of Anangarágá[1], the daughter of a brother of the King of the Nágas[m], who lives by herself in a palace in the forest, two months' journey from here. And what her beauty is, you yourself partly know by personal experience of the effect which even in a picture it produced upon you: yet what picture could be equal to the reality? For every one that sees her instantly falls in love with her, and many swoon away, as you did, and there are some who have even died. And yet the Creator, when he made her a casket of beauty so inimitably lovely, placed within it a heart of adamant, so hard, that it laughs at all the efforts of the flowery-arrowed god to pierce it. For innumerable suitors have sought her in marriage, coming from all the quarters of the world, and she receives them all with scornful indifference, yet entertains them magnificently for twenty-one days, on this condition, that every day

[1] *i.e.* 'the passion, or the rosy-blush, of love.' (Pronounce the two first syllables to rhyme with 'among,' with a north-country g.)

[m] These Nágas are beings of serpent nature, but often confounded with men: *e.g.* in *Kathá Saritságara*, I. 6, the nephew of the King of the Nágas is said to be a Brahman. Their women are of inconceivable loveliness.

they ask her a riddle[n]. And if any suitor should succeed in asking her something that she cannot answer, then she herself is to be the prize; but if within the stipulated time he fails, then he becomes her slave, to be disposed of how she will. And no one has ever yet succeeded in asking her anything she cannot answer; for she is of superhuman intelligence, and learned in all the sciences; but of the countless suitors who have tried and failed, some she has sent away, and others she retains about her person as slaves, pitilessly showing them every day that beauty which is for ever unattainable to them, so that their lot is infinitely worse than that of beasts. And therefore, O King, I warned you, lest the same thing should happen also to you. O be wise, and shun her, before it is too late. For I think that no lot can be more wretched than that of those who are doomed to everlasting regret, for having lost what nevertheless they see ever before them, as it were within their reach.

Then King Súryakánta laughed aloud, and he

[n] Very few of the stories are really riddles, but they all give the Princess an opportunity of displaying her ready judgment and acumen. It will also be seen, that owing to the device with which the story concludes, there are really only nineteen days, instead of twenty-one.

said: Painter, your judgment is not equal to your skill in your own art. For there is a lot infinitely more miserable, and it is that of one who passes his whole life in regret for an object which, with daring and resolution, he might have attained. Let me rather pine for ever miserable in the contemplation of such beauty, than weakly abandon my chance of enjoying it. Then the King gave that painter three crores of gold pieces, as the price of the portrait of the Princess, which he took away from him; and, after allowing him to paint his own portrait, dismissed him. And he said to his ministers: Make all ready: for this very night I start in quest of the Princess Anangarágá. Then his ministers deliberated together, and said to each other: Certainly, if the King should fail in his object and never return, the kingdom will be ruined. Yet, the same will be the case if he remains here, and scorning the society of all other women, never has a son. Therefore it is better as it is. For of two evils, the least is a good. Moreover, he may possibly succeed.

So that very night, burning with the fierce fire of impatience, the King transferred the burden of his government to the shoulders of his ministers, and set out, with the portrait of his beloved, to win or lose her. And he would have taken nobody with him.

But as he was preparing to depart, his boon companion, Rasakósha [o], said to him: Sire, would you go alone? And the King said: My friend, I may fail, and never return. Why should I drag others with me into the jaws of destruction? I will go by myself. Then Rasakósha said: King, what are you about? You leave yourself behind, if you leave me. That half of you which inhabits your own body is altogether gone upon [p] the Princess, and wholly intent upon her, so as to think of nothing else: then how will you baffle her, without that other half of you which lives in me, and is always ready for your service? And what am I to do without my better half? And even if you *do* fail, what will you do without me? for even prosperity without a friend is tasteless [q]: how much more adversity! Then the King said: Well, be it so. Come, let us be off. But Rasakósha said: Did I not say that your mind

[o] Pronounce *Russakósh.* The name refers to the part he will play in the story: it means both 'a ball of mercury,' and 'a treasury of taste, wit, literary sentiments or flavours,' a sort of walking encyclopædia. The King's companion is a salient figure in Hindoo drama: he is a sort of Sancho Panza, *minus* the vulgarity and the humour.

[p] This colloquialism is an exact facsimile of the Sanskrit expression.

[q] A play upon his own name.

was wandering? Would you start on such a perilous adventure, without first securing the aid of Winá-yaka[r]? Who ever succeeded in anything that neglected him? And the King said: It is true. In my eagerness I had almost forgotten him. So he praised Ganésha, saying: Hail, O thou lord of the Elephant Face, whose trunk is uplifted in the dance! Hail to thee, before whom obstacles melt away like the mists of night before the morning sun! Hail to thee, aided by whom even the weak triumph over the strong! Hail to thee, without whom all prudence is vain, and all wisdom, folly! Hail, O thou whose basket ears flap like banners of victory in the wind!

Then they set out on their journey. And they fared on day and night through the forest, full of wild beasts, apes, and Shabaras[s] as the sea is of jewels: but the King in his preoccupation for many days neither spoke nor ate nor drank, living only on air and the portrait of the Princess, which night and day he devoured with his eyes.

Then one day, as they rested at noon beneath the thick shade of a *Kadamba*[t] tree, the King gazed for a long time at the portrait of his mistress. And

[r] Ganésha, the god of obstacles and success. See Day 1.

[s] An old name for Bhíls and other wild tribes.

[t] 'A tree with orange-coloured fragrant blossoms.'

suddenly he broke silence, and said: Rasakósha, this is a woman. Now, a woman is the one thing about which I know nothing. Tell me, what is the nature of women? Then Rasakósha smiled, and said: King, you should certainly keep this question to ask the Princess; for it is a hard question. A very terrible creature indeed is a woman, and one formed of strange elements. *Apropos*, I will tell you a story: listen.

In the beginning, when Twashtri[u] came to the creation of woman, he found that he had exhausted his materials in the making of man, and that no solid elements were left. In this dilemma, after profound meditation, he did as follows. He took the rotundity of the moon, and the curves of creepers, and the clinging of tendrils, and the trembling of grass, and the slenderness of the reed, and the bloom of flowers, and the lightness of leaves, and the tapering of the elephant's trunk, and the glances of deer, and the clustering of rows of bees[x],

[u] The Hindoo Vulcan, sometimes, as here, used for the Creator, *dhatri* = Plato's δημιοῦργος. Sanskrit literature is the key to Plato; much of his philosophy is only the moonlike reflection of Hindoo mythology.

[x] Hindoo poets see a resemblance between rows of bees and eye-glances.

and the joyous gaiety of sunbeams, and the weeping of clouds, and the fickleness of the winds, and the timidity of the hare, and the vanity of the peacock, and the softness of the parrot's bosom, and the hardness of adamant, and the sweetness of honey, and the cruelty of the tiger, and the warm glow of fire, and the coldness of snow, and the chattering of jays, and the cooing of the *kôkila*[y], and the hypocrisy of the crane, and the fidelity of the *chakrawáka;* and compounding all these together, he made woman, and gave her to man. But after one week, man came to him, and said: Lord, this creature that you have given me makes my life miserable. She chatters incessantly, and teases me beyond endurance, never leaving me alone: and she requires incessant attention, and takes all my time up, and cries about nothing, and is always idle; and so I have come to give her back again, as I cannot live with her. So Twashtri said: Very well: and he took her back. Then after another week, man came again to him, and said: Lord, I find that my life is very lonely since I gave you back that

[y] The Indian cuckoo. The crane is a by-word for inward villainy and sanctimonious exterior. The *chakrawáka*, or Brahmany drake, is fabled to pass the night sorrowing for the absence of his mate and she for him.

creature. I remember how she used to dance and sing to me, and look at me out of the corner of her eye, and play with me, and cling to me; and her laughter was music, and she was beautiful to look at, and soft to touch: so give her back to me again. So Twashtri said: Very well: and gave her back again. Then after only three days, man came back to him again, and said: Lord, I know not how it is; but after all, I have come to the conclusion that she is more of a trouble than a pleasure to me: so please take her back again. But Twashtri said: Out on you! Be off! I will have no more of this. You must manage how you can. Then man said: But I cannot live with her. And Twashtri replied: Neither could you live without her. And he turned his back on man, and went on with his work. Then man said: What is to be done? for I cannot live either with or without her[1].

And Rasakósha ceased, and looked at the King. But the King remained silent, gazing intently at the portrait of the Princess.

And thus travelling on, day by day, through the forest, at length they drew near to the palace of the Princess Anangarágá.

[1] The very echo of Martial.

DAY I.

THEN, when the towers of the palace rose over the trees, and gleamed like gold on their eyes in the beams of the morning sun, King Súryakánta suddenly exclaimed: Ha! I am undone. And Rasakósha said: How is that? Then the King said: Alas! I have been absolutely possessed by the image of my beloved, night and day, waking and sleeping, so that I have thought of nothing in the world beside. And now here we are at the end of our journey, but at the beginning of difficulties. For as to what I shall ask the Princess, I have not the shadow of an idea. And if the thought of her has such power to bewilder me at a distance, the sight of her will utterly deprive me of my reason, so that I am lost already. Then Rasakósha said: O King, this is exactly why the Princess has hitherto baffled all her lovers. The spell of her beauty robs them of their intellect, and chains up their invention, and thus they fall an easy prey. But fortunate are you, that while your best half has been absent from its body, your other half[a] has

[a] *i.e.* Rasakósha himself. The allusion is to a power, possessed by adepts in Yóga, of detaching the soul from the body. See Day II.

been watching over the empty case. Be under no concern: but when we are introduced into the presence of the Princess, tell her that you speak by my mouth, and leave all to me. So the King was relieved, and dismissing all other subjects from his mind, he again became wholly immersed in meditating on his mistress.

Then drawing nearer by degrees, at length they entered the precincts of the palace. And there they were met by warders, who enquired who they were. And they went and announced to the Princess that King Súryakánta had arrived as a suitor for her hand. So she sent chamberlains and others, who conducted the King to a pleasure-house of white marble in a garden beautiful with a lake and crystal baths, shady with trees, perfumed with breezes loaded with the fragrance of flowers, and musical with the songs of innumerable birds. There they passed the day. But the King, consumed with the fever of his burning desire to see the Princess, had neither eyes nor ears for anything but the portrait.

And when the sun set, King Súryakánta and Rasakósha went to the palace of the Princess, and entered the hall of audience, whose floor, inlaid with slabs of dark-blue crystal, reflected their feet, and whose walls flashed back from the facets of their jewels the light of innumerable lamps. And there they saw Anangarágá, sitting on a golden throne, clad in a robe of sea-green, and a bodice studded with coral, looking like Lakshmi [b] fresh from ocean. And her eyes were as long as a row of bees, and their lashes jet black with collyrium, and her lips were like freshly painted vermilion, and from her high bosom came the fragrance of sandal. And round her slender waist was a girdle of gold, and on her wrists and ankles gold bangles and anklets, and the soles of her little feet were red with lac, and in her black hair was a gold tiara in the form of a snake, with eyes of rubies, and a tongue of emerald. And in the radiance of her beauty she looked scornfully at the King, and, turning away her head, said, without waiting to be addressed: Propose your question. But the King, struck by the thunderbolt of her stupefying loveliness, sank mute and trembling upon a couch opposite to her, and gazed at her like a bird fascinated by a serpent. Then Rasakósha came forward, and prostrated himself at her feet, and said: Lady, this unworthy mortal is the King's mouth. Is it permitted him to speak?

[b] The goddess of fortune and wealth, who was churned up out of the ocean, and according to some, appeared reclining on an open lotus. Coral is one of the nine gems.

So the Princess said: Proceed. Then Rasakósha rose up, and stood before her, and began:

Lady, there lived formerly, in a certain country, a Chárwáka [c], who was about to be married. And while he was making preparations for the ceremony, one of his friends came to him, and gave him advice, saying: Propitiate Ganésha, in order that nothing untoward may occur to interfere with your marriage. Then that Chárwáka laughed in derision, and replied: My good Sir, you are a fool. Do I not know that knaves and fools invented the *Wédas*, and instituted the sacrificial rites for their own advantage? All these foolish tales about the gods are merely the dreams of madmen, or the livelihood of rogues. As for this Ganésha that you speak of, what is the use of him? Or how can there be a man with the head of an elephant? And what has he to do with success? He, who forms his plans with prudence, and executes them with wisdom, may count on success. Out on your Ganésha! I will ensure my own success.

So he spoke, but that lord of the Elephant Face heard him, and laughed to himself, gently waving

[c] *i.e.* an atheist. The opinions of this philosophical school may be found sketched in the *Sarwa-Darshana-Sañgraha*, § 1.

his trunk. And the Chárwáka went on with his preparations. But when all was ready, and the lucky day fixed, then on the morning of that day Ganapati spoke to a certain cow that used to wander at will about the streets, saying: Cow, go and drop your sacred excrement on that Chárwáka's doorstep. And the cow went and did so. And when the Chárwáka came forth from his house, he put his foot on the cow-dung, and slipped and fell, and broke his leg. So they took him up and carried him in again. And before his leg was cured, his bride died.

Then his friend came to him again, and said: See what comes of neglecting to worship Ganapati. But the Chárwáka answered: Go to; you are an idiot. Who could possibly foresee that a miserable cow would cast its dung on my doorstep? What has Ganapati to do with it? Does he, forsooth! look after and direct the excretions of all the cows in the world? A pleasant idea, to be sure! So saying, he drove his friend away, refusing to listen to him. And when his leg was well, he found another bride, and made preparations for another marriage. And he hired a band of sweepers to go before him and sweep all clean before his feet. But when the day came, Ganapati sent for a crow that eat the daily offerings, and said to him: Crow, there is a Chárwáka going to be married to-day. Now, there is an arch over a certain street, beneath which he will pass: and on it there is an image of myself, of stone, which is very old, and the rain and heat have loosened and cracked it, so that it is on the point of falling. Do you watch, therefore, and when you see the Chárwáka passing under, then seat yourself upon me, and I will fall. So the crow flew off, and watching his opportunity, seated himself upon the stone image of Ganapati; and it fell on the Chárwáka as he passed below, and broke his arm. So they took him up and carried him back to his house. And before his arm was well, his bride died.

Then his friend came once more to him and said: Is this your wisdom? What did I tell you? Is it not plain now, who it is that is thwarting your efforts? Then the Chárwáka flew into a rage, and said: Enough of your babbling! I will get married in spite of Ganapati. But what can be anticipated in this miserable city, whose cows befoul the streets, and whose buildings are tumble-down. I will provide against any similar accident happening again. So when he was well, he discovered another bride, and again made preparations for his wedding. And he arranged to go to the bride's house by a circuitous route outside the walls of the city, avoiding the streets altogether. But on the morning of the day, Ganapati went to Indra, and said: Wajradhara[d], there is a Chárwáka going to get married to-day. But he must pass over a certain water-course, which is now dry. Lend me your rain-clouds, for I must teach this infidel a lesson. So Indra sent his clouds, and rained furiously on the hills. And as the Chárwáka was passing over the water-course, the river rose suddenly, and swept down in torrents from the hills and carried him away and drowned him.

And Ganapati saw it and smiled. But on a sudden he wept violently.

Now tell me, Princess, why did the lord of obstacles laugh and weep? And Rasakósha ceased. Then the Princess answered: He laughed when he thought of the folly, blindness, and insolence of that miserable infidel. But suddenly great pity came over him, when he remembered the terrible punishment that awaited that foolish fellow in the future, and all those who like him prepare by their own actions a fearful retribution in other lives and another world: and so he wept[e].

[d] 'Wielder of the thunderbolt,' an epithet of Indra, the god of rain.

[e] Perhaps only a Hindoo could appreciate the dexterity with

And when the Princess had said this, she rose up and went out, dismissing the King without looking at him, with a wave of her hand: and the King's heart went with her. But the King and Rasakósha returned to their own apartments.

DAY 2.

THEN the King said to Rasakósha: My friend, although the Princess has answered your question, and you have lost me a day, yet I forgive you, for the sake of the wave of her hand which she made as she went away. Oh! it resembled the bowing of a blossom-loaded spray of creeper in a breeze. But if it were not for the portrait, it would be utterly impossible for me to endure the torture of separation from her till to-morrow. And he passed the night in a state of intoxication [f], drunk with the beauty of the Princess, gazing incessantly at the portrait. And he said: Certainly, this painter was master of his art. This is no picture, but a mirror.

which this story is placed first, and thus the favour of Ganapati, as it were, secured for the rest.

[f] Just as the clothes of the Princess change colour every day, so does the state of the King's mind, which goes through a regular series of transitory emotions (*wyabhichári*).

There is the very scorn on her lip. And when at last the sun rose, the King rose also, and passed the day with Rasakósha in the garden, longing for the moment of reunion. Then when the sun set, they went again to the hall of audience. And there they saw the Princess, clad in a red robe, with a bodice studded with pearls, and her crown and other ornaments, sitting on her throne. And the King trembled as she looked at him, and he sank upon a couch, speechless and fascinated, gazing at her loveliness. Then Rasakósha came forward, and standing before her, began again:

Lady, once upon a time there lived, in the country of a king called Dharmásana[g], an old Brahman who had three sons. And he possessed nothing in the world but nineteen cows. And when he was about to die, he called his sons around him, and said to them: My sons, I am in the mouth of death, therefore listen attentively to what I am going to say. All that I have to give you is these cows. Divide them amongst you; and let the eldest of you take half of them; and the next, a quarter of them; and the youngest, a fifth part of them. But

[g] *i.e.* 'seat of justice.' The meaning is important, as the sequel shows. It does the Princess credit that she notes and remembers it.

if there should be any remainder left over, you must all three of you eat it; if not, all the cows are to be given to the King, and my curse will rest upon you, for disobedience to my last wishes. And having said this, that old Brahman died. And his sons performed his obsequies, and burned him in accordance with the rites.

Then they assembled together for the division of the property. And the eldest brother said: Half of these cows, that is, nine cows and a half, are mine. And the next brother said: One quarter of these cows, that is, four cows and three-fourths of a cow, belong to me. Then the youngest said: One-fifth of these cows, that is, three cows and four-fifths of a cow, are mine. Then the eldest said: But the sum of all these, added together, amounts only to eighteen cows and a fraction. Thus there will remain over a portion of the last cow. And in that case we must eat it. But how is it possible for Brahmans to eat the flesh of a cow? Or even, how are we to take various portions of any cow, and leave it still alive[h]? But then, what is to be done? For unless we share in our due proportions, all the cows are to go to the King, and our father's

[h] To kill, let alone to eat, a cow, would be of course one of the most deadly sins of which a Brahman could be guilty.

curse will fall upon us. And yet what can have been the meaning of our father in placing us in so terrible a dilemma? Thus they disputed among themselves, and the day passed away, but not the difficulty, and night found them still arguing without any solution of the matter.

Now, Princess, tell me, how is this to be settled, so as to satisfy equally the father, the three brothers, and the King? And Rasakósha ceased. But the Princess bent down her head, and remained a moment in meditation, while the King's soul almost quitted his body. Then after a while, raising her head, she replied: Let the brothers borrow another cow. Then of the twenty cows, let the eldest take half, or ten cows; the next, a quarter, or five cows; and the youngest, a fifth, or four cows. Then let them return the borrowed cow. Thus the nineteen cows will be exhausted without leaving a remainder, and the father satisfied: each brother will receive more than under their own division; and finally, the King will be pleased. For he was a just King: and what could displease such a king more than that, in his dominions, Brahmans should kill and eat cows, or disregard their father's orders[1]. Rather

[1] See *Manu*, II., 227, *sqq*.

would he lose, not nineteen cows, but ten millions [k].

And when the Princess had said this, she rose up and went out, casting a glance, as she went, at the King, whose heart went with her. But the King and Rasakósha returned to their own apartments.

DAY 3.

THEN the King said to Rasakósha: My friend, though the Princess has answered your question, and yet another day has been lost, yet I forgive you, for the sake of the glance she gave me as she went away. Oh! it was cooling to my burning soul as the drops of rain to the parched and thirsty earth. And but for the portrait, it is certain that my life could not last till the morning. Thus the King lamented, and passed the night in a state of longing, gazing at the portrait of his beloved. And when at last the sun rose, he rose also, and passed the day with Rasakósha in the garden, longing for the moment of reunion. And when the sun set, they went again to the hall of audience. And there

[k] I remember to have heard a very inferior version of this story from an old Pundit with whom I read Maráthi.

they saw the Princess, clad in a yellow robe, and a bodice studded with diamonds, and her crown and other ornaments, sitting on her throne. And she looked intently at the King, who sank upon a couch, speechless and fascinated, gazing at her loveliness. Then Rasakósha came forward, and stood before her, and began again :

Lady, in a former age there was a king who died of a fever. And his heir was a baby, too young to speak or walk. Now that king had a brother, who desired the kingdom for himself. And in order to compass this object, he determined to make away with the little Rájá, thinking to himself : There will be no difficulty in this, for he is but a baby, and can easily be put to death in a thousand ways.

So one night he persuaded the child's attendants, by means of an immense bribe, to leave him alone in his room. And he hired an assassin to kill him, posting him in a secret place within the palace, and telling him : At such an hour, enter the king's room, where you will find him alone, and kill him. But this assassin was a Rajpoot from the Deccan, who had but just come to that city, and did not know who the king was. And expecting a man, at the appointed hour he entered the king's room, and saw nothing but a baby playing on the floor with a fruit. And the fruit, escaping from its hands, rolled to the feet of the assassin as he came in. And the little Rájá put out his hand, and cried, *Bhó, Bhó.* So the assassin rolled it back, and the baby laughed and clapped its hands. Thus they remained, playing with the fruit, till the guards came in and found that assassin. And when they asked him who he was, he said : I have a message from my master to the king. Then they laughed, and said : The king is dead : there is the king. But he was amazed, and said : Then I must return and tell the news to my master. For how can I deliver a message to one who cannot even speak? And they suffered him to depart, and he went out, and fearing for his own life, left that city without delay.

Then the king's brother, finding that his plot had failed, hired a whole band of robbers. And watching his opportunity, he posted them by the side of a road leading to a temple, and said : There will come by this road a baby, magnificently dressed, and ornamented with jewels, attended by servants. Fall on them and plunder them, and if you please, kill them, but make sure that you kill the baby. But while they waited, in the meanwhile some other robbers, attracted by the richness of the little Rájá's ornaments, set upon his retinue. And killing all his servants but one, who fled naked, they stripped the little Rájá of all he had on him, but left him alone alive, saying: He cannot tell any one, let him live. So they hastily departed. Then that fugitive crept back, and finding the baby in the road, picked it up, and wrapping it in a cloth, carried it home. And he passed before the eyes of the gang that was waiting to kill the baby Rájá, but they thought that he was some beggar, and took no notice of him. And thus a second time the child escaped.

Then the king's brother bribed a cook, who put deadly poison into the little Rájá's milk. And it was given to him in a crystal goblet. And he took it in both hands, and put it to his mouth, to drink; and at that instant, one of the attendants standing before him sneezed. And the little Rájá dropped the goblet, and began to crow and clap his hands in delight; but the goblet fell to the ground and broke into a thousand pieces, and all its contents were spilled upon the floor. Thus he escaped the third time. And before the king's brother could form another plot, he was himself slain by the husband of a woman of the Kshatriya caste, whom he had carried off and dishonoured.

Now tell me, Princess, how was it that the schemes of that villain could never succeed against the little king, being but a mere child? And Rasakósha ceased. Then the Princess said: It was its very childhood that baffled him. For just as a stone, lying openly on the ground, is more secure than a costly jewel, though protected by adamantine bars, because it is worthless and arouses no cupidity; so is a thing so feeble that none would attack it more powerfully protected by its very feebleness than strength possessed of many enemies though defended by a thousand guards. No antidote so good, as the absence of poison: no virtue so good, as the absence of beauty: no fortification so good, as the absence of enemies: and no guard so potent as the helplessness of a child. For where are the enemies of the fragile lotus?

And when the Princess had said this, she rose up and went out, looking back as she went at the King, whose heart went with her. But the King and Rasakósha returned to their own apartments.

DAY 4.

THEN the King said to Rasakósha: My friend, your question was again answered by the Princess, and of my days now three are gone, yet freely do

I forgive you, for the sake of the glance she gave me as she went away. Oh! it snared my soul as it were in a net. And but for the portrait to keep me alive during the period of separation, beyond question I should never see the light of day. So he passed the night in a state of lovelorn recollection[1], an enemy to sleep, gazing at the portrait. And when the sun rose, he rose also, and got somehow or other through the day, by the help of Rasakósha and the garden. Then when the sun set, they went again to the hall of audience. And there they saw the Princess, clad in a sable robe and a bodice studded with sapphires, and her crown and other ornaments, sitting on her throne. And she looked kindly at the King, who sank trembling upon a couch, speechless and fascinated, under the spell of her beauty. Then Rasakósha came forward, and standing before her, began again :

Lady, there lived formerly in a certain country two brothers, Brahmans, called Bimba and Pratibimba[m], who were twins. And I think that the Creator, when he made one, had gone under water to make the other. For the moon does not more closely resemble her own image in a lake, nor one

[1] *Smara* means both love and memory.

[m] Both words mean *image, reflection.*

leaf on a branch another, than each of them did the other. Between them, when they were children, the sole point of distinction was the charm tied for that purpose round their necks; and when they grew up, those who saw them together imagined that their own eyes had become enemies, and were each giving a separate reflection of the self-same object. And as their external forms, so were their voices, and their internal dispositions: they corresponded in every atom, from the extremity of the skin to the inmost recesses of the heart.

Now one day it happened that Bimba saw a young woman[n] at the spring festival. And she looked at him at the same moment. And then and there the god of love penetrated their hearts, employing their mutual glances as his weapon. So having discovered her family and place of residence, Bimba used to go and visit her three days in every week. But in the excess of his own happiness, proud of the extraordinary beauty of his love, he could not contain himself, nor endure to keep the secret of his own good fortune. So he told his brother the whole story; and contriving a suitable opportunity, he exhibited to him his mistress, who was all uncon-

[n] The *hetæra* plays in old Hindoo stories a still larger part than she did in Greek.

scious of what he was doing. But Pratibimba, being as he was but the double of his brother, instantly conceived an equally violent passion for her. And without scruple—for what has love to do with honour?—he used to go himself, on the other three days of the week, to visit her. But she in the meanwhile, believing him to be Bimba himself, for she could not see any difference, only rejoiced in gaining as she thought the company of her lover twice as often as before.

But when some time had passed by, it fell out that Bimba, not being able to endure separation, went to visit his mistress on one of his brother's days. And when he got there, he saw Pratibimba, who had arrived before him, and was lying asleep on a couch while his beloved fanned him with a palm leaf. But she, when she saw Bimba come in, uttered a shriek of astonishment and terror, which woke Pratibimba. And while she looked in amazement from one to the other, Bimba rushed upon Pratibimba, mad with jealousy and howling with rage, while Pratibimba did the same to him. And grappling with one another, they rolled upon the floor, fighting and kicking each other, till, hearing the shrieks of the woman, the King's officers came in and separated them, and carried them all three to the judge. Then Bimba said: This man is my brother, and he has stolen my beloved from me. But Pratibimba said: No, she is mine: it is you that are the thief. Then Bimba howled: I was first, and you are a villain. And Pratibimba echoed his words°. So the judge said to the woman: Which of them is your lover? But she answered: Sir, I cannot tell which is which, nor did I ever know that there were two till to-day.

So now tell me, Princess, how shall the judge distinguish between them? And Rasakósha ceased. Then the Princess said: Let him take all three apart, and ask each to describe in detail the circumstances under which he saw the woman first. For though the impostor may have heard that it was at the spring festival, yet the eye that saw, aided by the heart that remembers, will convict the ear that only heard.

And when she had said this, the Princess rose up and went out, smiling at the King over her shoulder, and she drew away the King's heart after her. But the King and Rasakósha returned to their own apartments.

° There is an untranslateable play on the word here.

DAY 5.

THEN the King said to Rasakósha: My friend, though my mistress guessed your question, and now four days have gone, yet I forgive you, for the sake of the smile she gave me when she went away. Oh! it irradiated the gloom of my soul like as the moonlight illuminates the forest glades: and when she disappeared, darkness again prevailed. But for the portrait, I were a dead man before morning. And he passed the night in a state of impatience, gazing at the portrait. Then when the sun rose, he rose also, and passed the day by the help of Rasakósha and the garden. And when the sun set, they went again to the hall of audience. And there they saw the Princess, clad in a pale red[p] robe, and a bodice studded with emeralds, and her crown and ornaments, sitting on her throne. And she dropped her eyes when she saw the King, who sank with a beating heart upon a couch, speechless and fascinated, under the spell of her beauty. Then Rasakósha came forward and stood before her, and began again:

Lady, in former times there was a king, who made

[p] *Goura* cannot mean white, because *dhawala* comes on a later day.

war upon a neighbouring king, and went out and fought a great battle with him. Now there was in his army a certain Kshatriya, who, fighting all day long in that battle, after slaying multitudes of the enemy with his single arm, at length grew tired and faint from exhaustion. And perceiving this, many of the enemy set upon him at once, and overpowered him, and after mangling him with innumerable wounds, left him for dead upon the ground. But when the moon rose, that Kshatriya recovered his senses, and as it were came back to life. And he dragged himself with difficulty as far as a neighbouring village. And then his strength failed, and sinking down exhausted at the door of a certain house, he struck one great blow upon it, and fell down senseless.

Now there lived in that house a Brahman woman, whose husband was away from home. And she was beautiful as a jasmine blossom, and pure as snow, and her name was Suwarnashílá [q]. And hearing the knock, in the dead of night, she was frightened; but she looked out of a small round window, and saw in the bright moonlight a man lying still at her door. Then she thought: This may be a snare. Alas!

[q] See below.

the neighbours praise me for my beauty, and to whom is not beauty an object of cupidity? Or how can beauty, like a great pearl, be safe when its guardian is away? Then she looked again, and saw a dark stream trickling from the body along the white ground. And her heart was filled with compassion, and she thought: Doubtless the man is wounded, and perhaps dying. The greater[r] sin would be, to leave him to die at my door. So she summoned her maid, and went out, and took in the wounded man, and dressed his wounds and nursed him, keeping him in her house till he was well.

Then that Kshatriya, seeing her daily, was burned to a cinder by the glory of her beauty, and he made evil proposals to her. But she stopped her ears, and would not listen to him, but said: What! would you repay benefits with treachery and ingratitude? Know, that to a virtuous woman her husband is a god. Depart, and let me alone. Then finding that he could not prevail upon her, the Kshatriya said to her: It is you, not your husband, that is the divinity. Your beauty would turn even a holy ascetic from his penance. And though I owe you my life, yet you

[r] i.e. to take him in, with her husband away, would be bad enough, but, &c. A Hindoo even at the present day would murder his wife for a much smaller crime than this.

have robbed me of it again. And now I must depart quickly, otherwise my passion will master me, for love is stronger than gratitude. Then he went away hurriedly, but with reluctance, somewhere else.

But when the husband returned, a certain barber's wife, who was jealous of Suwarnashílá for her beauty, met him and said: Happy are those who possess treasures. In your absence another man has been wearing your crest-jewel. So the husband, burning with jealousy, went home and asked his wife. And she said: It is true, but listen; and she told him the whole story. But he would not believe her. Then she extended her hand to the fire, and said: I appeal to the fire, if I have ever been faithless to you for a moment, even in a dream. And the fire shot up, and a bright flame licked the roof, and two tongues of flame crept out and kissed that saint, one on the mouth, and the other on the heart. But blinded with jealousy and rage, the husband said: This is a trick. And taking his sword, he said to his wife: Follow me. So she said: As my lord pleases. Then he led her away into the forest, and there he tied her to a tree, and cut off her hands and her feet, and her nose and her breasts, and went away and left her. And after a while she died alone in the forest, of cold and pain and loss of blood.

But that Kshatriya heard of what he had done. And filled with rage and despair, he went to that husband, and said to him: O fool, know, that you have murdered a saint. And but that I know that life will henceforth be a punishment to you worse than any death, I would slay you where you stand. But as it is, live, and may your guilt bring you death without a son. Then the husband, learning the truth, and discovering the villainy of that lying barber's wife, was filled with remorse. And he abandoned the world, and went to the Ganges to expiate his guilt. But the Kshatriya killed himself with his own sword.

So now tell me, Princess, why does fate inflict such terrible punishment on the innocent[s]? And Rasakósha ceased. Then the Princess said: Can emancipation be attained, save by those who are worthy of it? And how can gold[t] be tested, save by fire? And Suwarnashílá stood the test, and proved her nature: and doubtless she has her reward. For even death is not so sure as the consequences of even the minutest action.

[s] This appalling question, which has puzzled the wise men of all ages, is answered by the Princess as well as by any one else.

[t] An allusion to the name Suwarnashílá, which means 'good as gold.'

Then a bodiless voice [u] fell from the sky, and said aloud: Well spoken, dear child. And the Princess rose up and went out, looking at the King with glistening eyes, and the heart of the King went with her. But the King and Rasakósha returned to their own apartments.

DAY 6.

THEN the King said to Rasakósha: My friend, though your question was again answered by the Princess, and now five days are lost, yet fully do I forgive you, for the sake of the tear that glistened in her eye as she went away. O! it was like a drop of dew in the blown flower of a blue lotus. It is beyond a doubt that but for the portrait my life would fail before the morning. And he passed the night in a state of stupefaction, gazing at the portrait of his mistress. Then when the sun rose, he rose also, and got through the long hours of day with difficulty by the help of Rasakósha and the garden. And when at length the sun set, they went again to the hall of audience. And there they saw

[u] This is an everyday phenomenon in Hindoo stories; and its appearance in the *Golden Ass* of Apuleius puts it beyond all doubt that his story came originally from India.

the Princess, clad in a blood-red robe and a bodice studded with opals, and her crown and other ornaments, sitting on her throne. And she was looking for the King when he came in, and the King sank upon a couch, speechless and fascinated, under the spell of her beauty. Then Rasakósha came forward and stood before her, and began again:

Lady, there was once a king who had three queens, of such indescribable beauty, that at night in the light fortnight it was impossible to decide which of the four was the true moon. And one night, when the king was sleeping in the hot season on the terrace of his palace in the company of his queens, he woke up while they were asleep. And rising up, he stood in the moonlight looking down upon his sleeping queens. And he said to himself: Various indeed is the form assumed by the beauty of woman. But I wonder which of my queens is the most beautiful of the three. So he went from one to the other, considering them attentively. And one queen lay on her back in the full light of the moon, with one arm over her head, and one breast raised, and every now and then a light breeze stirred and lifted her garment, disclosing it. And another lay in the shadow of the trellis-work with alternate stripes of shadow and light turning her into curves of ebony and ivory. And the third lay all in deep shadow, save that a single streak of moonlight fell softly on the shell of her little ear. So the king wandered all night from one to another, puzzling over his difficulty, thinking each queen to be the most beautiful till he came to another. And before he had decided it, the sun rose.

Then when, after performing his daily ceremonies, he was going to take his seat on his throne, his prime minister, named Nayanétri[1], said to him: O king, why are your royal eyes red with want of sleep? So the king said: Nayanétri, last night it came into my head to ask myself, which of my three queens was the most beautiful. And I could not sleep for my perplexity, and even now I have not been able to solve the problem. Then Nayanétri said: O king, be content that you have queens between whom there is no distinction in beauty, and no cause of jealousy. Idle curiosity destroys peace of mind and produces evil. But the king said: I am determined, at whatever cost, to settle this point.

So finding that the king's heart was set upon the matter, Nayanétri said to him: King, ministers

[1] A master of policy.

are like riders: a horse which they cannot restrain they must at any rate guide, or it will be the worse for both. Since it is absolutely necessary for you to decide between your queens in respect of beauty, listen to me. There has recently arrived in your capital a dissolute young Brahman called Kántígraha[y], who is famous in the three worlds as a judge of female beauty. Send for him, and let him see your queens, and he will certainly tell you which is the most beautiful. For a swan cannot more accurately separate milk from water[z], than he can distinguish the shades of beauty.

Accordingly the king, much pleased, had Kántígraha fetched; and as they stood conversing, he caused his three queens to pass in order through the room. And when the first queen passed, the Brahman stood as if rooted to the ground. And when the second passed, he trembled slightly. And when the third passed, he changed colour. Then when all had gone, the king said: Brahman, tell me, for you are a judge, which of those three is

[y] Meaning both 'a *connoisseur*,' and 'a devourer of beauty,' with an allusion to Ráhu, who causes eclipses by devouring the moon.

[z] A fabled power of swans, frequently alluded to in Sanskrit poetry.

the most beautiful? But Kántígraha said to himself: If I tell the king, I may displease him, by slighting his favourite: moreover, the other two queens will certainly hear of it, and have me poisoned. So he bowed, and said: King, I must have time to decide: give me leave till to-morrow. So the king dismissed him. And Kántígraha went quickly away, intending to quit that city before nightfall, yet with reluctance, for he said to himself: There is one of those queens I would give much to enjoy.

But Nayanétri, who could read the heart from the external signs, said to the king: King, this Brahman means to give you the slip, for he is afraid, and will probably endeavour to leave the city before night. But I can tell you what to do, so as to discover his opinion. So the king did as his minister told him. And discovering which of his queens was the most beautiful, he loved her the best, so that the other two, being jealous, poisoned her. And the king, discovering it, put them to death. Thus through curiosity he lost all his queens, as Nayanétri predicted.

So now tell me, Princess, what did the king do to discover the opinion of Kántígraha? And Rasakósha ceased. Then the Princess said: He need not have done anything: the third queen was the most beautiful. For the first queen's beauty astounded that Brahman; that of the second struck him with awe: but that of the third touched his heart. However, Nayanétri wished to make sure. And so, knowing the character of Kántígraha, he caused the king to send him false letters, one from each queen, feigning love and appointing a meeting, but all for the same hour. And he, being only one, would go to that queen whom he judged most beautiful, and be caught by the guards set to watch by the king. For the actions of men are a surer indication of their hearts than their words.

And when the Princess had spoken, she rose up and went out, with a look of regret at the King, whose heart went with her. But the King and Rasakósha returned to their own apartments.

DAY 7.

THEN the King said to Rasakósha: My friend, though the Princess has again baffled you, and now six days are lost, yet I forgive you, for the sake of the opportunity that your story gave my beloved of exhibiting her wonderful intelligence. Oh! she has the soul of Brihaspati in a woman's body. But my heart was racked by the regret in her glance as she went away. And even with the .portrait, I cannot understand how I shall endure the period of separation. So he passed the night in a state of restlessness, gazing at the portrait. And when the sun rose, he rose also, and managed to get through the day, aided by Rasakósha and the garden. Then when the sun set, they went again to the hall of audience. And there they saw the Princess, clad in a robe of azure and a bodice studded with crystal, and her crown and other ornaments, sitting on her throne. And she sighed when she saw the King, who sank upon a couch, speechless and fascinated, under the spell of her beauty. Then Rasakósha came forward and stood before her, and began again :

Lady[a], there was in former times a rogue, who had lost his all by gambling with other rogues like himself, and who became an ascetic in order to make a living by seeming piety. So he smeared his body with ashes, and matted his hair into a knot, and put on a yellow rag and a necklace of bones and a rosary, and went about hither and

[a] Should any reader be of opinion that I ought to have omitted or emasculated this story, I can only reply that I wish all Bowdlerisers no worse fate than that of the ascetic in the text.

thither in the world practising hypocritical asceticism when anybody was looking at him, and begging. And one day, when he was sitting by the roadside, the daughter of the king of that country passed by on her elephant. And the wind blew aside the curtain of her *howdah*, and revealed her to his eyes. And she struck him with the fever of fierce desire, so that he uttered an ejaculation, and exclaimed: The fruit of my birth certainly lies in obtaining possession of that beauty. But how is it to be done?

So after meditating profoundly on the matter for a long time, he went to a large tree just outside the king's palace, and hung himself up like a bat [b], head downwards, from a branch. And thus he remained for hours, muttering to himself. And this he continued to do every day, so that the people came in crowds to see him. And news was carried to the king that a great ascetic had come, and was practising penance in a tree in front of his palace. So the king, much pleased, and thinking himself fortunate, went to examine him, and the

[b] History repeats itself. M. Rousselet, who travelled in India in the sixties, mentions, in his *L'Inde des Rajas*, a case that he saw in Rájputána of a holy man who suspended himself in a tree 'like a ham.'

ascetic blessed him, upside down, from the tree. Then the king was delighted, and sent food and other offerings to the rogue.

Then one day it happened that the king's daughter, whose name was Hasamúrtí [c], came by on her elephant, and saw the ascetic hanging like a bat in the tree. And the sight tickled her, and she laughed aloud; and the ascetic heard her. So getting down from the tree, he went to the king. And having effected an entrance, he said to him: King, your daughter laughs at me, thus disturbing my devotions in the tree. Now in former times many great sages, irritated by scorn or neglect, have cursed the offenders, and inflicted terrible punishments on them. But I am long-suffering, and will spare your daughter. Nevertheless, I am about to curse your kingdom, so that no rain will fall on it for twenty years. Now the king was a great simpleton. And when he heard this, he was dreadfully alarmed: and he prayed so earnestly to the ascetic that the rogue, pretending to be mollified, said: Well, for this time I will abandon my design of cursing your kingdom. Only beware that it does not occur again. Then

[c] *i.e.* 'laughter incarnate.'

he went back to his tree, and the king scolded his daughter in private.

But the very next day the king's daughter passed again by the tree. And seeing the ascetic hanging, in spite of her promises to her father, her former hilarity returned upon her mind, and she laughed louder and longer than before. So the ascetic went again to the king, who, pale with terror, managed with difficulty and the most abject apologies once more to appease his wrath. And he returned to his tree, and the king again scolded his daughter, who promised never to offend again.

Then for two days Hasamúrtí went and came by another road, to avoid the opportunity of giving offence to the ascetic. But on the third day she forgot, and once more came past the tree, and saw him hanging. And suddenly, as if inspired by Shiwa himself[d], she burst into a peal of laughter, and she continued to laugh as if she was mad, even after she had entered the palace.

So the ascetic got down from the tree, and went to the king. And he said: O king, certainly your

[d] *Attahása*, 'loud laughter,' is a name of Shiwa. Kálidás (in his *Cloud*, v. 62) compares the snowy peaks of Mount Kailas to the laughter of Shiwa 'rolled into a ball.' (Note, that laughter is always *white* in Sanskrit poetry.)

kingdom is doomed, and your daughter is possessed by an evil spirit. For she has laughed at me again, even worse than before, and cancelled years of my reward, by disturbing my meditations. Now, therefore, prepare to suffer the extremities of my vengeance. Then the king, at his wits' end, said: Holy man, is there absolutely no remedy? The ascetic replied: Am I ever to be disturbed in my devotions? There is none; your daughter is clearly incurable. But the king said: Can nothing be done to cure her? Do you know no potent spell to conquer her malady? Then that rogue, inwardly delighted, said: Well, I will do this, out of mercy. I will see your daughter, and perform incantations over her. And if I can drive out the evil spirit of unseasonable laughter that possesses her, it is well: but if not, nothing remains but the curse.

So the king carried him to his daughter's apartments, and said to his daughter: My daughter, your laughter incessantly disturbs this holy man at his devotions. And now he has come, out of mercy, to exorcise the laughing demon that possesses you: otherwise, my kingdom, cursed by him, will perish for want of rain. Then the ascetic said: Let all others depart, and leave me in private with the king's daughter. But the king said aside to the ascetic: Sir, my daughter must not be left alone with any man. Then the ascetic replied: Fear nothing on my account: I am not a man: it is many years since I sacrificed my manhood [e] to the Dweller in the Windhya hills.

But Hasamúrtí heard him, and she said to herself: My father is a fool, and doubtless this man has some design against my honour. He shall find I can do more than laugh. So she said to her father: Have no fear: this is a holy man. But she secretly stationed all her maids in readiness in the next room. Then when the ascetic found himself alone with the king's daughter, his evil passion rose to such a pitch that he could scarcely contain himself. Nevertheless he drew a circle, with trembling hands, and placing the king's daughter in it, he muttered awhile, and then said: My daughter, you must have the quarters of heaven for your only garments [f], or the spell will not work. Remove your clothes. But Hasamúrtí said: Reverend Sir, it is impossible. Then he caught hold of her. But she clapped her hands, and her maids

[e] *Spado factus sum.* The 'dweller' is Párwatí, or Durgá, Shiwa's other half, in the strict sense of the term.

[f] *Digambara*, *i.e.* you must be stark-naked, or in a state of nature.

ran in and seized him. And she said: Examine this ascetic, and see whether he is a man or not. So they did so, and said, laughing: Madam, he is very much a man indeed. Then Hasamúrtí said: Take this knife, and deprive him of his manhood. And they did as she commanded them.

Then Hasamúrtí said to him: Now go, for the incantation is finished. And if you please, complain to the king, my father: I have the evidence to convict you. So the maids released that ascetic. But he, as soon as they let him go, began to laugh, and continued to laugh till he reached the king. And he said: O king, do not hinder me: we have successfully performed the incantation, and see, I have caught the laughing demon, and am carrying him away. And he went away laughing, with death in his heart.

So now tell me, Princess, why did that ascetic laugh? And Rasakósha ceased. Then the Princess, frowning slightly, replied: He laughed, in the cowardice of his soul, with exultation at having escaped from those maids as from the mouth of death: counting the failure of his scheme and the loss of his manhood as nothing, in comparison with the preservation of bare life. For cowards count the loss of life as the greatest of evils: but the great-souled esteem it as the least, and would forfeit it a thousand times, rather than fail in the object at which they aim.

And when she had said this, the Princess looked significantly at the King, and rose up and went out, and the King's heart went with her. But the King and Rasakósha returned to their own apartments.

DAY 8.

THEN the King said to Rasakósha : My friend, though my beloved has answered your question, and now seven of my days are gone, yet I forgive you, not only for the sake of her frown—oh ! it played on her face like a dark ripple over the surface of a lake—but still more for the sake of her words. For surely she meant to encourage me in my suit. Oh ! she is a pạragon of wisdom, and yet it is just her wisdom that makes her inaccessible. Even the portrait scarcely suffices to keep my soul alive during the long hours of separation. Thus he passed the night in a state of trepidation, gazing at the portrait. And when the sun rose, he rose also, and got somehow or other through the day by the help of Rasakósha and the garden. Then when the sun set, they went again to the hall of audience. And there they saw the Princess, clad in a saffron robe and a bodice studded with carbuncles, and her crown and ornaments, sitting on her throne. And she smiled at the King as he came in, and he sank upon a couch, speechless and fascinated, under the spell of her beauty. Then Rasakósha came forward and stood before her, and began again:

Lady, there lived formerly in a certain country a very stupid Brahman householder, who inadvertently committed a deadly sin. And his spiritual adviser told him, that his guilt could be cleansed and his sin atoned for, only by going and spending the remainder of his life bathing in the Ganges. So he handed over his goods to his son, and set out, with his pot and staff, on his pilgrimage to the Ganges. And after travelling for some days, he came to the bank of a small mountain streamlet, whose waters in the hot season were all but dry. And he said to himself: Doubtless this is the sacred Ganges. So he took up his abode on the banks of that stream, bathing every day in such water as he could find. And thus he remained for five years.

Then one day there passed by that way a Páshupata[g] ascetic. And he said to the Brahman: My son, what are you doing here? So he replied: Reverend Sir, I am performing penance, for the expiation of sin, on the banks of the Ganges. Then the ascetic said: What has this miserable puddle to do with the Ganges? And the Brahman said: Is this, then, not the Ganges? And the ascetic laughed in his face, and said: Truly, old as I am, I did not think that there had been folly like this in the world. Wretched man, who has deluded you? The Ganges is hundreds of miles away, and resembles this contemptible brook no more than Mount Méru resembles an ant hill.

Then the Brahman said: Reverend Sir, I am much obliged to you. And taking his pot and staff, he went forward, till at length he came to a broad river. And he rejoiced greatly, saying: This must be the sacred Ganges? So he settled on its bank, and remained there for five years, bathing every day in its waters. Then one day there came by a Kápálika[h], who said to him: Why do you remain here, wasting precious time over a river of no account or sanctity, instead of going to the Ganges? But the Brahman was amazed, and said:

g A particular follower of Shiwa.

h Another sect of Shiwa worshippers.

And is this, then, not the Ganges? Then the Kápálika replied: This the Ganges! Is a jackal a lion, or a Chándála[1] a Brahman? Sir, you are dreaming.

Then the Brahman said sorrowfully: Worthy Kápálika, I am indebted to you. Fortunate was our meeting. And taking his pot and staff, he went forward, till at length he came to the Nermada. And thinking: Here, at last, is the sacred Ganges; he was overjoyed; and he remained on its banks for five years, bathing every day in its waters. But one day he observed on the bank near him, a pilgrim like himself, casting flowers into the river, and calling it by its name. So he went up to him and said: Sir, what is the name of this river? And the pilgrim answered: Is it possible that you do not know the holy Nermada? Then the Brahman sighed deeply. And he said: Sir, I am enlightened by you. And he took his pot and staff, and went forward.

But he was now very old and feeble. And long penance had weakened his frame and exhausted his energies. And as he toiled on in the heat of the day over the burning earth, the sun beat on his

[1] The lowest of all the castes, a synonym for all that is vile and impure, like the 'Jew dog' of the Middle Ages.

head like the thunderbolt of Indra, and struck him with fever. Still he gathered himself together and struggled on, growing weaker and weaker day by day, till at last he could go no further, but fell down and lay dying on the ground. But collecting all his remaining strength, with a last desperate effort he dragged himself up a low hill in front of him. And lo! there before him rolled the mighty stream of Ganges, with countless numbers of pilgrims doing penance on its banks and bathing in its stream. And in his agony he cried aloud: O Mother Ganges! alas! alas! I have pursued you all my life, and now I die here helpless in sight of you. So his heart broke, and he never reached its shore.

But when he got to the other world, Yama said to Chitragupta[k]: What is there down against him? And Chitragupta said: I find against him a terrible sin. But that he has expiated by fifteen years' penance on the banks of Ganges. Then that Brahman was amazed, and said: Lord, you are mistaken. I never reached the Ganges. And Yama smiled.

Now tell me, Princess, what did Yama mean by his smile? And Rasakósha ceased. Then the Prin-

[k] Yama (pronounce Yum) is the judge of the dead, and Chitragupta his recorder, who keeps account of every man's actions

cess said: Yama is just, and cannot err: and Chitragupta cannot be deceived. But what is this whole world but illusion! And just as penance performed in an improper spirit, even on the actual banks of Ganges, would be no true penance, so that poor simple Brahman's penance, performed in the belief that he had reached the Ganges, was counted by that holy One as truly so performed. For men judge by the fallacious testimony of the senses, but the gods judge by the heart.

And when the Princess had said this, she rose up and went out, smiling at the King, whose heart went with her. But the King and Rasakósha returned to their own apartments.

DAY 9.

THEN the King said to Rasakósha: My friend, the Princess is again victorious, and now eight days are lost, yet I cannot but forgive you, for the sake of the smile she gave me when she went away. Oh! it gleamed on my soul like the dazzling whiteness of a royal swan illuminated by the sun on the Mánasa lake. Alas! even the portrait will scarce enable me to live till the morning. And the King passed the night in a state of bewilderment, gazing sorrowfully at the portrait. Then when the sun rose, he rose also, and got through the long day by the help of Rasakósha and the garden. And when the sun set, they went again to the hall of audience. And there they saw the Princess, clad in a purple robe, with a bodice of burnished gold, and her crown and ornaments, sitting on her throne. And she looked at the King with joy, and the King sank upon a couch, speechless and fascinated, under the spell of her beauty. Then Rasakósha came forward and stood before her, and began again:

Lady, in a certain city there was a wealthy merchant, who possessed a very beautiful wife; and he loved her more than his own soul. But she was of light conduct, and walked in a path independent of her husband[1], and looked after other men, and her virtue under temptation was like a blade of grass in a forest conflagration. And though out of his great love for her, that merchant forgave her all her faults, she only despised him for it, and disliked him the more.

And one day, she looked out of her window, and saw in the street a handsome young Rajpoot. And smitten with passion, she instantly left her husband

[1] An independent woman is a synonym for a harlot, in Sanskrit.

and her home, and ran away with him. But when he found that she had gone, that merchant, her husband, in his despair almost abandoned the body. But the hope that she would one day return kept him alive: hope alone binds those whom separation has made miserable to the world. Nevertheless, from the day she departed, all other things became abominable in his eyes. And neglecting his business, he sank into poverty, and became an object of contempt and derision to his friends. And forsaking all occupation or pleasure, he remained alone in his empty house, with the image of his runaway wife in his heart, night and day. And thus he lived for three years, every hour of which seemed to him as long as a *kalpa*, in the black darkness of desolation.

But she, in the meanwhile, after living with that Rajpoot for some time, grew tired of him, and left him for another paramour, and him again for another, flitting from one to another like a bee from flower to flower. And it happened that one night, when she was living with a certain merchant's son, he, in the new ardour of his admiration for her beauty, suddenly stooped down to kiss her feet. But not being aware of his intention, she drew her foot abruptly away, and it caught on the jewel of a ring in his ear, and was torn. And even though it was cured, the scar remained.

And one day, when three years had gone by, her husband, the merchant, was sitting by himself in his deserted house, gazing with the eye of his heart [m] at the image of his wife, when there came a knock at the door. And as his servants had all long ago left him, for he had no money to give them, he went to open it himself. And when he did so, he looked, and there before him was his wife. She was worn, and old, and the flower of her beauty was gone, and she was clothed in rags and dusty with travel, and she looked at her husband with eyes dim with tears and shame and fear, as she leaned against the doorpost, faint from hunger and thirst and fatigue. But when he saw her, his heart stopped, and his hair stood on end, and he uttered an exclamation of wonder and joy. And taking her in his arms, he carried her in, and put her on the bed which she had abandoned and disgraced; and fetching food and water, with feet that stumbled from the ecstasy of his joy, he washed the dust off her, and dispelled her anxiety and fear, and revived her heart, and uttered no reproaches, but blessed

[m] *Smara* means 'love' and also 'memory.'

her for her return, with laughter and tears; and it was as though she had never been away, even in a dream. And as he was gently cherishing her, and shampooing her all over to soothe her fatigue, his eye fell on the scar that had remained on her foot from the wound caused by the merchant's son. And putting his finger on it, he said to her with a smile of compassion: Poor wounded foot, it has found a resting-place at last. But she looked at him silently, with large eyes, and suddenly she laughed, and then and there her heart broke and she died. And he, when he found that she was dead, fell down on the floor at her feet, and followed her.

So now, tell me, Princess, why did that woman's heart break? And Rasakósha ceased. Then the Princess said: It broke with grief. For when she saw that her husband repaid her evil conduct with kindness, and remembered the occasion that had caused that wound upon her foot, repentance came suddenly and flowed into her, like a river too great for her heart to hold it, and it split and broke, and she died.

And when she had spoken, the Princess rose up and went out slowly, looking regretfully at the King, whose heart went with her. But the King and Rasakósha returned to their own apartments.

DAY 10.

THEN the King said to Rasakósha: My friend, now nine days are gone, and I begin to fear: and certainly, I never will forgive you if I lose my darling. For she looks at me now, not as she used to look, but kindly, as if she also felt the pang of separation. Now, therefore, devise some cunning question that she cannot answer, while I endeavour by means of the portrait to keep my soul from parting from my body till to-morrow. So the King passed the night in a state of doubtful perplexity, gazing at the portrait. And when the sun rose, he rose also, and got somehow through the day, aided by Rasakósha and the garden. And when the sun set, they went again to the hall of audience. And there they saw the Princess, clad in a robe of dazzling white, and a bodice studded wfth amethysts, and her crown and other ornaments, sitting on her throne. And she looked at the King and drew a long breath, and the King sank upon a couch, speechless and fascinated, under the spell of her beauty. Then Rasakósha came forward and stood before her, and began again:

Lady [n], there lived formerly in a certain village,

[n] The point of this crafty little story almost evaporates in translation. It is artfully contrived to entrap the Princess

a tawny-haired wrestler, who kept in his house a pet. And one day he returned home and found that it had gone out. So he ran out into the street to look for it. And seeing a man sitting at the corner of the street, he asked him : Have you seen my pet ? The man said : Had it a string tied round its neck ? The wrestler said : Yes. Then the man said : It went this way. So the wrestler went on, and enquired again. And one said : I saw it standing on two legs, endeavouring to climb that wall. Then another said : And I saw it on all fours crawling along by the wall. And a third said : And I saw it, on three legs, scratching its head with the fourth. So going still further, he met a washerman, who told him : It came this way and made faces at its own face in the water. And going still further, he met a fruit-seller, who said : I saw it sitting under that tree, pulling out the feathers of a bleeding crow [o], and I gave it a handful of monkey nuts.

Then going on, he met two men conversing together, and he asked them. And one said : I saw it with another of its own species searching for fleas

into saying 'an ape :' but she is too cunning. Tawny-haired means, literally, 'ape-coloured.'

[o] The pun is untranslateable : it may mean also, 'tossing up its gory locks' (*kákapaksha*).

in its hair. And the other said: What was the colour of the hair[p]? The wrestler answered: The same as mine. So the other replied: It is over yonder in the tree, swinging on a branch.

So now tell me, Princess, what kind of creature was that wrestler's pet? And Rasakósha ceased. Then the Princess smiled and said: It was no ape, but a child; perhaps his own son.

And when she had said this, she rose up and went out, as if with difficulty, looking reproachfully at the King, whose heart went with her. But the King and Rasakósha returned to their own apartments.

DAY 11.

THEN the King said to Rasakósha: My friend, though the Princess is still unconquered, and ten of my days are gone, yet I would have forgiven you, had you not made this day's story so short. For no sooner had it begun than it ended; and now not only is my delight cut short, but, like a thirsty man who has drunk insufficiently, I have not had

[p] This is the critical point. These words may also mean: What is the caste of the child? The wrestler's answer fits both. The searching for fleas, as applied to the child, will surprise no one who has been in India.

enough to last me till I see my beloved again. At least endeavour to lengthen your stories, otherwise I am wholly undone. For now must I endure another night of separation, by the feeble aid of the portrait, which loses its power daily by contrast with the original. Thus the King spent the night in a state of fearfulness, gazing at the portrait. And when the sun rose, he rose also, and hardly got through the day with the assistance of Rasakósha and the garden. Then when the sun set, they went again to the hall of audience. And there they saw the Princess, clad in a robe of emerald hue, and a bodice studded with moonstones, and her crown and other ornaments, sitting on her throne. And she looked at the King affectionately, and he sank upon a couch, speechless and fascinated, under the spell of her beauty. Then Rasakósha came forward and stood before her and began again :

Lady, there lived formerly, in a certain country, a king. And he had a domestic chaplain, who was smitten with an evil passion for another man's wife. And she was a wicked woman and returned his love. But owing to the watchful jealousy of her husband, they could find no opportunity for private interviews. So at last, finding himself unable to visit his beloved in his own person, that chaplain adopted the following scheme. He feigned great friendship for her husband, and paid him many attentions. And being an adept in Yóga, he cultivated his good-will by exhibitions of his superhuman power. And one day he said to him: I know by my art how to enter other people's bodies, and I can cause you to do the same, if you have any curiosity about it. Than that foolish husband, not perceiving his intention; eagerly consented.

So the chaplain took him away one night to the cemetery, and there by means of spells and magic power he caused both of them to abandon the body. But no sooner had the husband quitted his body than the chaplain entered it himself. And without losing a moment, he hurried away, rejoicing in the success of his stratagem, to the house of his beloved in the form of her husband. But the husband, finding himself deprived of his own body, exclaimed: Alas! I am undone. But having no other resource he was obliged against his will to enter the body of the chaplain, which lay empty near him. And he returned slowly from the cemetery, full of grief, homewards. But as chance would have it, his mind being wholly occupied with other reflections, his feet led him as it were of their own accord to the house of the chaplain, whose body he was occupying.

In the meantime, his wife, consumed by the fever of desire, and unable any longer to endure separation, seized the opportunity afforded by her husband's absence, and went like an *abhisárikâ* [q], to the house of her Brahman lover. And so it happened, that when the chaplain arrived at her house, she was not there. So he remained there, cursing his fate, and devoured by impatience, all night long. But she on her part arrived at his house, just before her husband, in the form of the chaplain, came there also. And when he went in, he was astonished to see his own wife. But she, not recognising who he was, but imagining him to be her lover, ran towards him and threw her arms round his neck, exclaiming: At last I have you. And that foolish husband was so delighted, for for a long time his wife had treated him coldly, that he forgot everything in the joy of the moment, and remained with her all night, enjoying the company of his own wife.

Then in the morning she rose up early while he was still asleep, and went secretly back to her own house. And the chaplain, on his part, wearied out with waiting, and in a very bad humour, left

[q] A term, very common in Sanskrit poetry, for *a woman who goes of her own accord to her lover.*

her house before she arrived, and returned home. And when he got there, he saw, to his astonishment, the husband in his body, lying asleep on his bed. So he woke him and said angrily: What are you doing in my bed? Then the husband replied: What do you mean by running away with my body? The chaplain said: Enough of this! I have suffered the tortures of hell in your abominable body, and I have a good mind to burn it. So the husband trembled for fear, and said humbly: I had no body but yours to enter, and I was cold; give me back mine, and take your own as soon as possible. So the chaplain carried him away to the cemetery, and by his magic power caused them to quit their bodies, and each re-entered his own.

But no sooner had the husband got back into his own body than he woke as it were from a dream, and remembered all: and he exclaimed: Rogue of a Brahman, it was you my wife embraced. But the chaplain replied: What have I had to do with your wife? But mad with rage, the husband laid hold of him, and dragged him to the king's officers. And he fetched his wife, and told the judge the whole story, and said: Punish these wicked persons: for they have robbed me of my honour. Then the chaplain said: I have not touched your wife. And she said : Of what are you complaining? Was it not yourself that I embraced[1]? But the judge was puzzled, and did not know what to say.

Now, Princess, decide for him. And Rasakósha ceased. Then the Princess said : The chaplain was a rogue, and intended wickedness, yet he was not amenable to the pains of law; for though he had planned, he had not executed, his scheme. And the woman, though she had done wrong, yet did it under the eye and sanction of her own husband, who acquiesced in and approved of her act. But that husband, whose passions were so little under control that he could aid and abet his wife in soiling his own honour, well knowing what he was about, deserves nothing but contempt and derision as the author of his own misfortune. Therefore let all three be dismissed unpunished.

And when the Princess had spoken, she rose up and went out, reluctantly, and the King's heart went with her. But the King and Rasakósha returned to their own apartments.

[1] It is not clear how she knew this, unless she heard him tell the judge.

DAY 12.

THEN the King said to Rasakósha: My friend, though I hear but little of your stories, for the beauty of my beloved holds me spellbound and stops my ears, yet methinks her intelligence must be more than human, for as yet even you have not succeeded in posing it. And now eleven of my days are gone, and only ten remain. Never will I forgive you if I lose her. For day by day her looks grow kinder, and the moment of separation more appalling, and the efficacy of the portrait less potent to soothe me in her absence, so that it is doubtful whether I can live till to-morrow. And the King passed the night in a state of sickness, gazing at the portrait. And when the sun rose, he rose also, and passed the day with difficulty, aided by Rasakósha and the garden. Then when the sun set, they went again to the hall of audience. And there they saw the Princess, clad in a robe of rose colour, and a bodice studded with ox-eyes[8], and her crown and other ornaments, sitting on her throne. And she leaned eagerly forward to see the King come in, and he sank upon a couch, speechless and fascinated, under the spell of her beauty. Then

[8] It is not clear what *goméda* means.

Rasakósha came forward and stood before her, and began again:

Lady, there was once a lordly elephant, the leader of a forest herd. And he rushed through the forest, like a thunderbolt of Indra, and the rain of ichor poured down from his mighty temples in streams, as he broke down the bushes and young trees in his charge. And then, having sported to his heart's content, he marched slowly through the glades like a mountain, with his herd behind him. And coming to an ant-hill, he drove his tusks into it, and cast up the earth. And then going onward, he stood at rest in a little pool, and drenched his sides with clear water collected in his trunk: and running his tusks into a bank, he stood leaning against a lord of the forest[t], swaying gently to and fro, with his eyes shut, and his basket-ears cocked, and his trunk hanging down. And the ivory of his tusks showed against his great dark-blue body like a double row of white swans against a thunder-cloud.

But meanwhile, the ants were thrown into confusion by his destruction of their hill, which killed many thousands of them. And they said: What! are we to die for the wanton sport of this rogue

[t] *i.e.* a tall tree. Our idiom is the same.

of an elephant? So they determined to send a deputation to the elephant, to demand reparation. And they chose seven of the wisest among them. So the ambassadors went and crawled in a row up the bole of the great tree against which the king of the elephants was leaning, till they reached the level of his ear. Then they delivered their message, saying: O king of the elephants, the ants have sent us to demand reparation from you for causing the death of great numbers of their caste. If not, there is no resource but war. But when the elephant heard this, he looked sideways out of the corner of his eye, and saw the row of ants upon the trunk of the tree. And he said to himself: This is a pleasant thing. What can these contemptible little ants do to us elephants? And taking water in his trunk, he discharged it with a blast against them, and destroyed them.

But when the ants saw the destruction of their ambassadors, they were enraged. And waiting till night, they crept out of the ground in innumerable myriads while the elephants were asleep, and gnawed the skin of their toes and the soles of their feet, old and young[u]. Then when in the morning the

[u] The author probably knew that the elephant's feet are very apt to go wrong and cause trouble: but whether 'white

elephants began to move, they found their feet so sore as to be almost useless. So trumpeting with rage and pain they rushed about the forest destroying the ant-hills. But they could not reach the ants, who crept into the earth, while the more they ran about the worse grew their feet. So finding all their efforts useless, they desisted: and fearing for the future, they resolved to conclude peace with the ants. But not being able to find any, they sent a mouse, who went underground, and carried their message to the ants. But the ants replied: We will make no peace with the elephants, unless they deliver up their king to be punished for slaying our ambassadors. So the mouse went back to the elephants, and told them. And seeing that there was no help for it, they submitted.

Then the king of the elephants came alone into the forest, with drooping ears, to deliver himself up to the ants. And the ants said to the Shami[x] creeper: Bind this evil-doer, or we will gnaw your roots and destroy you. So the creeper threw its arms round the elephant, and bound him so tightly that he could not stir. And then the ants crawled

ants' or any other ants could produce the disease is a point for the natural historian to determine.

[x] Famous in poetry for its extraordinary toughness.

out in myriads and buried him in earth, till he resembled a mountain. And the worms devoured his flesh, and nothing but his bones and his tusks remained. So the ants remained unmolested in the forest, and the elephants chose another king.

So now tell me, Princess, what is the moral[y] of this story? And Rasakósha ceased. Then the Princess pondered awhile and said: Even united, the weak are not always stronger than the strong. For an elephant is still an elephant, and an ant but an ant. But the strength of the strong is to be estimated by their weakness[z]. For if the elephants had known this, and protected their feet, they might have laughed at all that the ants could do to them, and even a single elephant would have been more than a match for all the ants in the world.

And when the Princess had said this, she rose up and went out slowly, looking sorrowfully at the King, whose heart went with her. But the King and Rasakósha returned to their own apartments.

y Literally, what is the error of policy (*nítídósha*) in the story.

z *i.e.* 'a chain is no stronger than its weakest link.' The Princess's answer is exceedingly clever: and there are few who would not have given the obvious answer which she rejects.

DAY 13.

THEN the King said to Rasakósha: My friend, unless I am blinded by love and egoism, the Princess exhibits signs of a disposition to favour me. But alas! now twelve of my days are gone, and only nine remain. Oh beware! lest you lose me my beloved. And even the portrait now brings me no relief, for day by day it grows less like her. It looks at me with scorn, but she with tenderness. Even with it, I know not how I shall endure separation till the morning. So the King spent the night in a state of lassitude, gazing at the portrait. And when the sun rose, he rose also, and passed the long hours of day with the help of Rasakósha and the garden. Then when the sun set, they went again to the hall of audience. And there they saw the Princess, clad in an orange-tawny robe, and a bodice studded with rubies, and her crown and other ornaments, sitting on her throne. And a shadow fled as it were from her face when she saw the King, and he sank upon a couch, speechless and fascinated, under the spell of her beauty. Then Rasakósha came forward and stood before her, and began again:

Lady, once upon a time, the master of a caravan

was crossing the great desert. And as he went along, he suddenly looked up, and saw before him in the distance the walls of a great city, with a beautiful lake of heavenly blue before it. And he was amazed; and with a soul on fire with longing for the nectar of that lake and that city, he urged on his camels in that direction. But he could not reach it: and suddenly it disappeared, and he found himself alone in the desert, with the sun and the sand, and no water and no city. Then he said: This is a wonderful thing. I would not lose that city for all my wealth. Then his followers said to him: Sir, this is a delusion: it is the mirage: there is no such city and no water. But he would not believe them. And remaining where he was in the desert, he waited till next day. And at the same hour he saw it again. So he mounted his swiftest camel, and pursued it for hours far into the desert, but he could not overtake it: but as before, it disappeared.

Then he abandoned his journey and encamped in the desert. And day after day he gave chase to that beautiful city with its water, but never got any nearer to it. But the more he pursued it, the more his yearning to reach it grew upon him, so that at last he forgot everything else in the world.

And meanwhile his affairs went to ruin through neglect. And hearing of his proceedings his relations came to him in the desert, and said: What is this that you are doing? What madness has smitten you? Do you not know that this is the mirage, and that you are wasting your time in pursuing phantoms while your wealth goes to ruin? But he answered: What are words in comparison with the testimony of the eyes? Do I not see the city and its water as I see you yourselves? Then how can it be a delusion? Then his relations flew into a rage, and said: You fool, it is the mirage. But he said: If it is nothing, then how can I see it? Explain this to me. But they could not. So they abused him and laughed at him, and went away leaving him alone in the desert. And he remained there, spending his all in purchasing camels, and every day pursuing that city till it disappeared. And this he continued to do, till his wealth was exhausted, and his camels died, and he himself was lost and died in the desert, and the sun whitened his bones.

Then his story went abroad, and the people said: What difficulty is there in this? The sun of the desert made him mad. But his relations said: Out on this madman! he has destroyed us with his folly.

And a certain ascetic heard the story: and he laughed to himself, and said: *Trashy trishy washy wishy*[a]. Says the pot to the pipkin: Out on you, miserable clay!

Now tell me, Princess, what did that ascetic mean? And Rasakósha ceased. Then the Princess said: His relations blamed the madness of that caravan-leader, in that he took mirage for reality, not knowing that they were themselves no less mad, in taking this world and its perishable wealth for reality, and pursuing, as he did, phantoms. For what is this world but illusion? Thus they resembled pots of clay abusing clay pipkins for being made of clay.

And when the Princess had spoken she rose up and went out slowly, looking at the King sadly, and the King's heart went with her. But the King and Rasakósha returned to their own apartments.

DAY 14.

THEN the King said to Rasakósha: My friend, this day also is lost, and now but eight days remain behind. And each day the moment of separation

[a] I have slightly modified the original jingle, which means: The thirst for delusion is the bane of the universe.

becomes more terrible, and the period of absence more insupportable: while the virtue of the portrait wanes, like the moon, threatening to leave my soul in total darkness. And yet what is a single night of separation to the whole of my life, if I lose her! So the King passed the night in a state of anxiety, gazing at the portrait. Then when the sun rose, he rose also, and managed to get through the day with the help of Rasakósha and the garden. And when the sun set, they went again to the hall of audience. And there they saw the Princess, clad in a robe of cloth of silver, and a bodice studded with beryls, and her crown and other ornaments, sitting on her throne. And her bosom heaved when she saw the King, who sank upon a couch, speechless and fascinated, under the spell of her beauty. Then Rasakósha came forward and stood before her, and began again:

Lady, there was in former times a king, who collected rarities from all quarters, purchasing them at no matter what price: and his palace was the resort of merchants of every land, who flowed into it like the rivers into the sea. And one day there came a merchant, who said to him: O king, I bring you a thing which has not its peer for rarity or beauty in the three worlds. And I procured it for you, knowing your generosity, at the risk of my life. Then he took from a chest a cup, made of the tusk of an elephant, white as snow, but round its rim ran a blood-red ring. And he said: This is the cup out of which Bimboshthá [b], the daughter of the King of Lanka [c], a Rákshasi famous in the three worlds for her incomparable beauty, drank every day. So exquisitely is she formed that it seems as if the separate perfections of all other women have been collected together to make her members. But the apex and crest-jewel of all her charms is her mouth. The very soul of vermilion is pale compared with her lips; redder than blood themselves, they banish all blood from the faces of all who behold them, pallid with passion at the sight of them. And whatever she touches with them bears ever afterwards the stain, like the stain of fruit: and as you see, the edge of this cup has been turned by the touch of her lips to a colour which nothing in creation can parallel. And I bribed her doorkeeper to steal it, for an immense sum of money, and came away fearing for my life; and now it is a present to your Majesty. Then

[b] i.e. 'red lipped.'

[c] Ceylon: reputed to be the home of a certain kind of demons called Rakshasa.

the king, overjoyed by the singularity and extraordinary beauty of that cup, ordered his treasurer to pay to the merchant ten times the amount he had given the doorkeeper, and dismissed him.

But it happened that the king's son was present at their conversation, and heard what the merchant said. And an overpowering passion instantly came upon him for that lady of the ruddy lips. And thinking of nothing else, he went to bed at night, and fell asleep, and dreamed a dream. He thought that he mounted a horse, and rode without ceasing at full gallop, till he came to the shore of the sea. And there dismounting in haste, he entered a ship, and set sail for Lanka. And the ship carried him swiftly over the sea, and on arriving, he leaped out, and ran quickly through the streets, till he came to the palace of the daughter of the Rakshas. And as he reached it, that instant the sun set on one side of the sky, and the moon rose, like another sun, in the opposite quarter, and lit up with his [d] radiance all the front of the palace. And he looked, and lo! there on the terrace he saw before him that daughter of the Rakshas, illuminated by the amorous moon, whom she rivalled

[d] The moon is not feminine in Sanskrit.

in beauty; and on the yellow disc of her face her two lips shone like two leaves of fire. And the king's son, unable to bear the lustre of their beauty, fell down in a swoon. But in his swoon he saw before him those lips without intermission, and they swelled up till they became like two huge mountains, and then, breaking into innumerable pairs which filled the sky like the stars, they crowded in upon him, and he felt them gently kissing him all over. And on a sudden, he saw the palace again before him, and he entered it, and saw the daughter of the Rakshas at the end of a long hall, and he ran up to her and sank down at her feet. But she, bending over him, approached her lips to his cheek. And as they came nearer and nearer, they suddenly became a pair of hideous jaws, with lips thin and green as a blade of grass, and a double row of teeth white as ivory and sharp as saws, and a black pit between. And as they loomed larger and larger upon him out of the darkness, he uttered a loud shriek—and awoke.

So now tell me, Princess, why did that King's son shriek? And Rasakósha ceased. Then the Princess said with a smile: He was afraid of being bitten.

And when she had spoken, she rose up and went out, looking with longing eyes at the King, whose heart went with her. But the King and Rasakósha returned to their own apartments.

DAY 15.

THEN the King said to Rasakósha : My friend, that merchant was a liar ; for no lips in the world could match the beauty of those of my beloved. Alas ! that the sweetness of her smile should be the means of conveying such bitterness to my soul, as she answers your questions with unerring dexterity, and so annihilates my hopes each day. And now but seven days remain, and the thought of losing her is like poison in the draught of nectar which I drink daily from her beauty. Even the portrait is becoming hateful to me, for it mocks me with its scorn, and assuredly my life will be extinct before the morning. So the King passed the night in a state of wretchedness, gazing at the portrait. And when the sun rose, he rose also, and got somehow through the day, by the help of Rasakósha and the garden. Then when the sun set, they went again to the hall of audience. And there they saw the Princess, clad in a copper-coloured robe, and a bodice of burnished silver, and her crown and other ornaments, sitting on her throne. And her eyes sparkled when she saw the King, who sank upon a couch, speechless and fascinated, under the spell of her beauty. Then Rasakósha came forward and stood before her, and began again :

Lady, once upon a time a young and handsome bee, that had till then grown up at home and been fed by his parents, set out for the first time in his life on an expedition to fetch flower-nectar for the purpose of making honey. And attracted by its fragrance he flew to a red lotus, growing on a pool in the forest, and was about to drain her of her sweetness. But the lotus closed her flower, and would not let him enter, saying : O bee, you come here, after the manner of your *caste*, insolently pushing into me, and seeking to rob me of my nectar, expecting to get all for nothing. Learn that you must buy my nectar of me. Then the bee buzzed and said : What shall I give you for it? What is there that you can want? Is it not enough for you to blow and bloom on this pool, scenting the air? Then the lotus said: There is still something wanting. Out upon you, foolish bee! You, a bee, not to know what I want! Go away, and find out, and then come back to me, if you want any of my nectar.

Then the bee buzzed violently in anger, and flew

away, to find out what the lotus wanted. And he saw a beetle busily grubbing in the earth at the foot of a tree. So he said: O beetle, tell me what the lotus wants. But the beetle answered: What is a lotus to me? Go elsewhere; I have no leisure. So the bee flew off and saw a spider, building a web in a branch. And he asked him. And the spider said: What she wants is doubtless a fly. But the bee thought: It cannot be a fly. This spider judges others by himself. And seeing a cloud floating in the air above him, he flew up and asked it: O cloud, what does the lotus want? The cloud said: Rain-drops. So the bee flew back and offered water to the lotus. But she said: I get that from the cloud and from the pool, not from you. Try again. So he flew away, and saw a sunbeam playing on a blade of grass, and asked it what the lotus wanted. The sunbeam said: Warmth. So the bee flew back bringing with him a fire-fly, and tried to warm the lotus. But she said: I get warmth from the sun, not from you. Try again. Then the bee flew off again, and saw an owl blinking in a tree; and he buzzed in his ear and roused him, and said: O owl, tell me what the lotus wants. The owl said: Sleep. And the bee flew back, and said to the lotus: I will lull you to sleep by humming to you, and fanning you with my wings. But the lotus answered: I get sleep from the night, not from you. Try again.

Then the bee in despair flew away, crying aloud: What in the world can this niggardly and capricious lotus want of me? And as fate would have it, his cry was overheard by an old hermit, who lived in the forest, and knew the language of all beasts and birds. And he called to the bee, and said: O thou dull-witted bee, this is what the lotus wants: and he told him Then the bee was delighted, and flew away to the lotus, and gave her what she wanted. And she opened her flower, and he went in and stole her nectar.

Now tell me, Princess, what did the bee give the lotus? And Rasakósha ceased. And the Princess blushed[e], and said: He gave her a kiss.

And when she had spoken, she rose up and went out, without looking at the King, and the King's heart went with her. But the King and Rasakósha returned to their own apartments.

[e] This is not a strict translation. Hindoo ladies, as far as my experience goes, do not blush: they 'exhibit shame.' But as the emotion is clearly the same, I have employed the English equivalent.

DAY 16.

THEN the King said to Rasakósha in ecstasy and despair: My friend, though owing to the answer of the Princess five days only now remain to me, yet I would not have had to-day's answer otherwise for all my kingdom; and freely do I forgive you. Oh! her confusion when she spoke almost broke my heart in twain, and if I dared, I would venture to think that she does not view me with indifference. But alas! how am I to survive the period of separation! For all virtue has gone out of the portrait, and from snow to cool my fever, it has now become a fire to increase it. And the King passed the night in a state of apprehension, alternately gazing at and flinging aside the portrait. And when the sun rose, he rose also, and hardly managed to get through the day with the aid of Rasakósha and the garden. And when the sun set, they went again to the hall of audience. And there they saw the Princess, clad in a robe of pearl-grey, and a bodice studded with agates, and her crown and other ornaments, sitting on her throne. And she looked shyly at the King, who sank upon a couch, speechless and fascinated, under the spell of her beauty. Then Rasakósha came forward and stood before her, and began again:

Lady, outside the wall of a certain city there was an old sacred banian tree. And in its hollow root there lived a black cobra. And every day it used to come out and lie in the sun before the tree, coiled round upon itself, and the people brought it offerings of milk and sweetmeats.

Now in that city there lived a very rich jewel merchant, who had a very beautiful daughter. And she was very fond of gems and precious stones, of which she possessed a very great number. But there was one which she had not got, and that was the jewel in the head of a snake. And this she desired so much that she thought all her other jewels of no account in comparison with it. And she heard of the sacred cobra, and being filled with cupidity, she hired a man of the Dómba caste to go by night and kill it, and bring her the gem in its hood. And when she had obtained it, she considered that she had obtained the fruit of her birth, and she valued it above all her other jewels, and wore it incessantly as a crest-jewel in her hair.

But Wásuki [f] heard of the slaughter of his subject, and he was wroth, and determined to punish the criminal. So he assumed the form of a man, and went to that city. And he made enquiries, till at

[f] The king of the snakes.

length he discovered that a certain merchant's daughter possessed the hood-gem of a snake. Then the lord of snakes assumed the form of a young and handsome jewel merchant. And he hired a house, close to that of the jewel merchant, and giving out that he was travelling on business, he lived magnificently, and gave feasts and banquets to all whom he met. And becoming acquainted with that jewel merchant, he charmed him by his wealth and accomplishments, and gave him many rare and inestimable jewels. And finally, he asked him for the hand of his daughter in marriage. And the merchant joyfully consented, thinking that nowhere in the world could he find such another son-in-law. And when he told his daughter, she was beside herself with delight, for she had seen that young merchant from a window, and heard of his great wealth and accomplishments; and she thought she was going to get as it were the very ocean itself for a husband[g].

Then an auspicious day was chosen, and the preparations for the wedding went on: and every day the lord of snakes sent baskets of jewels to his bride, whose senses almost left her in her joy. And at

[g] i.e. 'the mine, or receptacle of jewels,' a common appellation of the sea.

last the day came, and the nuptial ceremony was over, and the bridegroom went with his bride into the nuptial chamber. And he lifted her on to the marriage bed, and called her by her name. And as she turned towards him, he approached her slowly, with a smile on his face. And she looked and saw, issuing from his mouth and disappearing alternately, a long tongue, thin, forked, and quivering like that of a snake.

And in the morning the musicians played to waken the bride and bridegroom. But the day went on, and they never came forth. Then the merchant, her father, and his friends, after waiting a long time, became alarmed, and went and broke the door, which was closed with a lock. And there they saw the bride lying dead in the bed, alone, and on her bosom were two small marks. And they saw no bridegroom. But a black cobra crept out of the bed, and disappeared through a hole in the wall[h].

So now, Princess, tell me, what was there in the

[h] The *dénouement* of this story has a most singular resemblance to that of Prosper Merimée's *Lokis*. But apparently he drew that admirable story (as he did his *Carmen* and his *Venus*) from older sources, of Lithuanian, Gipsy, possibly even Hindoo origin.

snake's hood-jewel to make that merchant's daughter so desirous of it? And Rasakósha ceased. Then the Princess said: The attraction lay not in the jewel itself, nor its magic properties. But in this that she had not got it. For this is the nature of women, that they make light of what they have, and sigh for what they have not got.

And when the Princess had spoken, she rose up and went out, looking at the King with a deep sigh, and the King's heart went with her. But the King and Rasakósha returned to their own apartments.

DAY 17.

THEN the King said to Rasakósha: My friend, all doubt is over: my doom is sealed: for the intellect of the Princess is invincible. And yet unless my desire blinds me, she intended that sigh to point at me the significance of her words. Oh! the fear of losing her almost deprives me of my reason, and breaking loose like a *must* elephant from every restraint I shall destroy you, as he does his friend the *mahout*, by the most terrible of deaths. And yet my own lot will be worse than any death: for I shall die by inches, starving in the sight of food. Out upon the portrait that has brought me to ruin, and on the painter that painted it! For now I see clearly that it is not in the least like her; for she is kind, and only compelled by destiny in the form of her own intellect to ruin hopes that she would perhaps otherwise encourage. So the King passed the night in a state of exhaustion, averting his gaze forcibly from the portrait. And when the sun rose, he rose also, and passed the day with difficulty in the garden, aided by Rasakósha. Then when the sun set, they went again to the hall of audience. And there they saw the Princess, clad in a robe of russet[i] and a bodice studded with amber[k], and her crown and other ornaments, sitting on her throne. And she looked at the King with eyes whose lids were red with want of sleep, and he sank upon a couch, speechless and fascinated, under the spell of her beauty. Then Rasakósha came forward and stood before her, and began again:

Lady[l], there was once a king, who laughed at his kingly duties, and passed his time in evil courses, lying in bed, neglecting Brahmans, drinking wine, hunting, and idling in the society of fair women. And whosoever ventured to remonstrate

[i] *Kapisha.* [k] *Trinamani*, a gem that attracts grass.

[l] This story is only the embodiment of an idea familiar to every Hindoo, but in the original it is very pithily told.

with him, him he straightway banished from his kingdom. And as time went on, he grew worse and worse, for dissatisfaction and satiety came over him, and the only refuge open to him from their torture lay in drowning reflection by still more abominable orgies.

Then it happened that one day he went a-hunting. And the ardour of the chase drew him far out of his way, so that when the sun fell, he was deep in the forest, far from his palace. And while he was considering where he should pass the night, he came upon the hut of an aged hermit. So leaving his followers in the forest, he remained in the hut of that hospitable hermit for the night. And after making his supper on roots and fruits, he lay down to sleep on a bed of leaves and *Kusha* grass.

And in his sleep he had a vision. He thought he found himself on the bank of a great river, lit up by the sun where he stood, but emerging from black darkness, and running into it again in a circle. And he held in his hand a seed. And digging a hole, he planted that seed, and watered it from the river, and it became a shoot, and grew rapidly into a tall tree. And the tree put forth leaves, and blossoms, and at last a single fruit. And the fruit grew larger and larger, til it was as big as a gourd: and it became green as an emerald, and then red as a ruby, and shone in the sun: and its weight caused it to sink down within reach of his hand. So he put out his hand, and plucked, and ate it.

And in an instant he saw a colossal hand stretched out of the darkness, and it grasped him and whisked him away, and suspended him over an abyss by a slender string. And looking down, he gazed into unfathomable depths, and looking up, he saw a vulture pecking at the string with its beak; and an icy chill froze his heart, while burning fire tortured his extremities, and black darkness enveloped him: and it seemed to him that infinite ages passed in each instant of ineffable agony. Then on a sudden he awoke with a cry, and saw only that old hermit standing in the moonlight that fell through the roof, meditating, and muttering to himself.

Then he lay down again on the bed, and slept and dreamed again. And again it seemed to him that he planted a seed, and watered it on the bank of that river: and again it became a tree, and put out leaves and blossoms and a fruit, which as before grew green and red, and sank down into his hand. And he plucked and ate it again. And in an instant, a feeling of inexpressible bliss flowed in upon his soul, and he sank into a deep sleep, and lay as if he were dead, till that old hermit roused him in the morning with the sun streaming in through the door of the hut.

Then that king went home and changed his ways.

So now tell me, Princess, why? And Rasakósha ceased. Then the Princess said: He was afraid. For the tree was the tree of his own evil actions, and the eating of its fruit the ripening of their consequences, dooming him to a punishment of which the agony he endured in his dream was but a faint shadow. But had he lived otherwise, and accumulated virtue rather than vice, he would have obtained ultimately the bliss of emancipation, resembling the deep sleep which came upon him and obliterated his individuality, the second time he slept.

And when the Princess had spoken, she turned and looked at the King with tears in her eyes, and rose up and went out, and the King's heart went with her. But the King and Rasakósha returned to their own apartments.

DAY 18.

THEN the King said to Rasakósha: My friend, now in very truth am I eating the fruit of my own crimes in a former birth, since four days only remain; and well did you say that I am suspended by the heels over an unfathomable abyss, with ice at my heart. For only too well do I see that the Princess will stand the test, seeing that the sharp arrows of your cunning questions rebound from her as if, instead of a jewelled bodice, she was clad in a coat of mail. And the nectar of the portrait has become a poison, which will certainly put an end to me before morning. So the King passed the night in a state of despondency, with his back to the portrait. And when the sun rose, he rose also, and hardly contrived to pass the day by the help of Rasakósha and the garden. Then when the sun set, they went again to the hall of audience. And there they saw the Princess, clad in a robe of Indian red[m], and a bodice studded with sea-gems, and her crown and other ornaments, sitting on her throne. And she looked at the King, and drooped her head like a flower, and the King sank upon

[m] *Lóhita.* The sea-gem is perhaps some kind of pearl.

a couch, speechless and fascinated, under the spell of her beauty. Then Rasakósha came forward and stood before her, and began again :

Lady, a certain lover was bewailing the death of his mistress, and he exclaimed: O Death, thou art strong; but O Love, thou art stronger. And it happened that Yama[n] heard him. So he said to the god who has a row of bees for a bowstring[o]: Hear what nonsense that foolish fellow is prattling. But Kámadéwa replied: It is not nonsense, but the truth. I am the stronger. So a dispute arose between them, as to which of them was the stronger. And after a while, Kámadéwa said: What is the use of talking? Let us put the matter to the test, and make trial of our power. And Yama said: So be it. And they chose for the subjects of their experiments three things: a hero, a *nyagródha*[p] tree, and the heart of a sage.

Then Yama went first to the tree, and smote its roots with death. But as fast as they died, the branches, inspired by Káma, let down roots from

[n] The god of death (pronounce Yum).

[o] Káma, or Kámadéwa, the god of love. His names are innumerable.

[p] 'Down-grower,' the banian, which lets down roots from its branches.

above, and they struck into the earth, and became new trunks, and grew up and produced new branches, which did the same continually. So after a while Yama was tired and stopped, and there was the tree as strong as ever.

Then Kámadéwa said: See, I have conquered. But Yama said: Wait and see. And he went to the hero, and struck him down when he was fighting in the front of the battle, and he died. But Smara[q] inspired the people of that country; and they mourned for that hero, and built him a splendid pillar; and poets sang his glorious deeds, and mothers called their children by his name, and they worshipped him as an incarnation of deity in the temples.

Then Kámadéwa said: See, again I have conquered. Acknowledge that I am the stronger. But Yama said: Wait and see. And he went to the sage, as he was practising terrible austerities in the forest, and struck his heart and killed it. But even as he did so, Desire sprang up in it[r] again ever anew, and ever fresh attachments to the objects of sense, and so the battle went on continually in the heart of that sage, as it alternately became

[q] A name for Love which also means memory.

[r] One of the common names of Love is 'the mind-born.'

dead to the world, and then again alive, and subject to the influence of the pleasures of mundane existence.

Then Kámadéwa said : See, once more I am proved to be the strongest. The victory is mine. Confess that you are beaten. But Yama said : For all that I am the stronger, and that lover was a babbler. And Kámadéwa laughed at him and mocked him.

So now tell me, Princess, which is the stronger? And Rasakósha ceased. Then the Princess turned very pale [s], and said in a low voice : Kámadéwa is cunning, and like a dishonest gambler, loaded his dice to win. For in particular instances and limited times, he appears to be the stronger. And therefore it was that he challenged Yama, knowing very well that all instances must of necessity be limited to a place and time. But nevertheless Yama is stronger than he. For he is unlimited, being Time itself without beginning or end [t], and that power,

[s] She turned pale, possibly because she saw that her love for the King must have an end : but still more probably because she was afraid of offending the God of Love by not deciding in his favour.

[t] *Kála*, Time, is another name for Yama. The answer of the Princess is clever in the extreme.

whose nature it is to be unsusceptible of bounds, can no more be exhibited by particular instances than the ceaseless flow of Ganges can be contained in a single jar.

And when the Princess had spoken, she rose up and went out, looking at the King with eyes of sorrow, and the King's heart went with her. But the King and Rasakósha returned to their own apartments.

DAY 19.

THEN the King said to Rasakósha: My friend, now I may offer water[u] to my happiness, and this is the beginning of the end. For three days only now remain to me, and these will assuredly follow in the footsteps of their predecessors, and so shall I[x]. Then will my sun set for ever. Alas! I read my fate in the sorrow that filled my beloved's eyes, as she looked at me like a frightened fawn. O that she were either less beautiful or less intelligent, for in the union of these two virtues lies my destruction. Away with the portrait, which burns me like a fire.

[u] i.e. it is all over with me. Water is offered to the spirits of departed ancestors.

[x] i.e. I shall fail in my suit, like the others. The following sentence is a play on his own name.

So the King passed the night in a state of delirium, paying no heed to the portrait. And when the sun rose, he rose also, and passed the day, half living and half dead, in the garden with Rasakósha. And when the sun set, they went again to the hall of audience. And there they saw the Princess, clad in a robe of cloth of gold and a bodice studded with turquoises, and her crown and other ornaments, sitting on her throne. And she looked at the King with eyes in which joy and grief fought for the mastery: and the King sank upon a couch, speechless and fascinated, under the spell of her beauty. Then Rasakósha came forward and stood before her and began again:

Lady, there was once a Brahman named Kritákrita [y], who neglected the study of the Wédas, and walked in the black path, abandoning all his duties [z], and associating with gamblers, harlots, and outcasts. And he frequented the cemeteries at night, and became familiar with ghosts and vampires and dead bodies, and impure and unholy rites and incantations. And one night, amid the flaming of funeral pyres and the reek of burning corpses, a certain

[y] 'Done and not done.'

[z] *Áchárabhrashta*, an apostate or decasted person. See *Manu*, I., 108.

Vampire[a] of his acquaintance said to him: I am hungry: bring me fresh meat to devour, or I will tear you in pieces. Then Kritákrita said: I will bring it, but not for nothing. What will you give me for it? The Vampire replied: Bring me a newly slain Brahman, and I will teach you a spell for raising the dead. But Kritákrita said: That is not enough. And they haggled in the cemetery about the price. At last that abandoned Brahman said: Throw in a pair of dice that will enable me always to win at play, and I will bring you the flesh you require. So the Vampire said: Be it so. Then Kritákrita went away, and knowing no other resource secretly murdered his own brother, and brought him to the cemetery at midnight. And the Vampire kept his word, giving him the dice, and teaching him the spell.

Then some time afterwards, Kritákrita said to himself: I will try the efficacy of this spell that the Vampire has taught me. So he procured the body of a dead Chandála[b], and taking it at the dead

[a] *Wétála*, an uncanny being, generally possessing magic powers, given to occupying empty corpses and devouring human flesh.

[b] The lowest caste, whose very proximity was pollution to a Brahman.

of night to the cemetery, placed it on the ground, and began to recite the spell. But when he had got halfway through, he looked at the corpse, and saw its left arm, and leg, and eye moving horribly with life, the other half being still dead. And he was so terrified at the sight, that he utterly forgot the rest of the spell, and leaped up and ran away. But the corpse jumped up also, and a vampire entered its dead half, and it rushed rapidly after him, shuffling on one leg, and rolling its one eye, and yelling indistinctly: *Underdone, overdone, undone*[c] *!* But Kritákrita fled at full speed to his house, and getting into bed lay there trembling. And after a while he fell asleep. And then suddenly he awoke, hearing a noise, and he looked and saw the door open, and the corpse of that dead Chándála came in, and shuffled swiftly towards him on its left leg, rolling its left eye, with its dead half hanging down beside it, and crying in a terrible voice: *Underdone, overdone, undone!* And Kritákrita sprang out of bed, and ran out by another door, and mounting a horse, fled as fast as he could to another city a great way off.

And there he thought: Here I am safe. So he

[c] This is all one word in the original, *únádhikákritamkritam*, 'what has been done is too little, too much, and not done at all.'

went day by day to the gambling hall, and playing with his dice, won great sums of money, and lived at his ease, feasting himself and others. But one night, when he was sitting among the gamblers in the gambling hall, throwing the dice, he heard behind him a noise of shuffling. And he looked round, and saw, coming swiftly towards him on one leg, the corpse of that dead Chándála, with its dead half rotting and hanging down, and its left eye rolling in anger, and calling out in a voice of thunder: *Underdone, overdone, undone!* And he rose up with a shriek, and leaped over the table, and fled away by an opposite door and left that city, and ran as fast as he could, constantly looking behind him through the forest for many days and nights, never daring to stop even to take breath, till he reached another city a long way off. And there he remained, disguised and concealed, as it were in a hole. But all the gamblers in that gambling saloon died of fear.

And after some time he again accumulated wealth by gambling in that city, and lived in extravagance at his ease. But one night, when he was sitting with an *hetæra* whom he loved, in the inner room of her house, he heard the noise of shuffling. And he looked round, and saw once more the corpse of that dead Chándála coming swiftly towards him on one leg, with its dead half, from whose bones the flesh had rotted away, hanging down, and its left eye blazing with flames of rage, calling out with a voice like the scream of Ráwana: *Underdone, overdone, undone!* Then that *hetæra* then and there abandoned the body in her terror. And Kritákrita rose up, and ran out by a door, which led out upon the balcony, while the Chándála hastened after him. And finding no other outlet, Kritákrita flung himself down into the street, and was dashed to pieces, and died.

So now tell me, Princess, what did that corpse mean by his words? And Rasakósha ceased. Then the Princess said: There is no difficulty in this. Woe to the feeble souls that have not courage to carry through what they have the presumption to begin! They do indeed either too little or too much, and are themselves their own undoing. For the strong in virtue avoid sin altogether: while the daring in vice face the consequences of their own conduct: those attain heavenly rewards, and these the good things of this world; but the coward souls who are too weak to be either virtuous or vicious are punished by that very weakness in the form of their consciousness of guilt, and lose both worlds.

And when the Princess had spoken, she rose up and went out, looking and yet as it were not looking at the King, whose heart went with her. But the King and Rasakósha returned to their own apartments.

DAY 20.

THEN the King said to Rasakósha: My friend, I have been bitten by the beauty of this incomparable woman as by a black cobra, and now the poison works. I have but two more days to live. For certain it is that her answer to your last question will be my sentence of death, and equally certain it is, that she will give that answer; for her intellect is like the edge of a sharp sword, which while it cuts the knot of the problem will at the same moment pierce me to the heart. And the King passed the night in a state of despair, leaving his bed untouched. And when the sun rose, he rose also, and went out alone into the garden, and wandered about, dreading the setting of the sun, yet longing for reunion with his beloved, till his soul was almost riven in twain with opposite emotions. And he reproached Wináyaka, saying: O thou of the Ruddy Trunk, I have been deceived by thee:

and instead of clearing my road to success, thou hast blocked it by an insurmountable obstacle in the form of this lady's piercing acuteness of understanding. And then he said : This is no time for despair. Let me not, like Kritákrita, leave my work half finished, but rather endeavour myself to discover some riddle that she cannot answer. And yet what hope is there that where Rasakósha has failed, I should succeed? For the Princess is not more skilful in answering his questions, than he in composing them, being as it were a very ocean of stories in human form. Or rather, no mortal, but only a god, could pose the ingenuity of this lovely lady. Then he prayed to Saraswatí, saying: O goddess of speech, my only refuge is in thy favour. O befriend me, and either cloud the mind of my beloved with temporary bewilderment, or else reveal to me some puzzle which she will be unable to answer. Truly, my puzzle is worse than hers.

And on the instant, Saraswatí put a thought into his heart. And he sprang up with a shout of joy, exclaiming: Ha! I am favoured. Victory to Saraswatí. The Princess is mine. And he ran quickly to find Rasakósha, whom he discovered buried in profound meditation on a story for the coming evening, and said: My friend, away with meditation.

Εὕρηκα[d]! I will myself propose a riddle to the Princess this evening. Then Rasakósha said: O King, I congratulate you. But still, in a matter of such importance, let us risk nothing by presumptuous confidence. So propound your riddle to me first that we may make trial of its difficulty. Then King Súryakánta laughed in delight, and said: Your very doubt shows that it is unanswerable. My own case is the very problem. I will go to the Princess, and ask her what I ought to do. And if she tells me, then I will ask her to-morrow what she tells me to-day: and if she does not tell me, then she is mine according to the terms of the agreement, to-day: and so in either alternative, the bird[e] is caged.

Then Rasakósha said with a smile: Victory to your Majesty. Truly wonderful is the power of love: like a stone it at once blunts and sharpens the edge of intellect. For it formerly blinded you to everything in the world, and now it has sharpened your sight so as to discover what has escaped us all this time, though lying as it were on the road before us. But unless I am deceived by the external signs, I predict that the god of love will also

[d] Literally, 'the object is attained.' [e] Here there is a pun.

blind the Princess; or rather, that she will throw herself gladly into the cage. For none are so easily caught as those who wish to be; and though the Princess has been adamant to my questions, she will be soft as a flower to yours.

Then in his impatience the King could hardly endure the remainder of the day, burning with desire to put his question to the Princess. But at last the sun set. Then Rasakósha said: O King, go you alone to the hall of audience. For my absence will do you more service to-day than my presence did before. There are cases, when a friend shows his friendship rather by his absence than his presence. *Apropos*, I will tell you a story: Listen. But the King said: My friend, this is no time for stories, even though told by you. And though I will go alone to-night, without you, yet know, that should I achieve success by the favour of Saraswatí and the Lord of obstacles, I shall nevertheless owe it to you rather than myself. For not only have you sustained my life daily, during the hours of separation, but your stories have been as it were a ladder, by which I have ascended step by step to the window of my beloved's chamber. And does not the lowest rung of the ladder contribute equally with the highest to the attainment of the summit of hope? Then Rasakósha laughed, and said: O King, it is well. Now go, and though you have not heard my story, yet I have attained in some measure the end I had in view in proposing it. For you have kept the Princess waiting, and expectation increases desire. Good luck be with you!

Then the King left him and went very quickly by himself to the hall of audience. And his right arm throbbed as he drew near the door, and rejoicing at the omen, he went in. And there he saw Anangarágá, clad in a robe of the hue of indigo [f], and a bodice rainbow-hued like the neck of a pigeon, and studded with yellow sunstones, and her crown and other ornaments: but she had left her throne, and come towards the door, and was looking with anxiety for the King. But when she saw him she blushed [g], and returned in confusion to her throne. And King Súryakánta went up to her, and fell down before her and took her by the hand, and said: Lady, there was once a King, who became suitor to a Princess, lovely like thyself, on this condition, that if he could ask her a question that she

[f] This has a meaning: see below. The sunstone is probably a topaz.

[g] See note, p. 88.

could not answer, she should be his. Now tell me, O thou lovely incarnation of wisdom, what should he ask her?

And instantly the Princess rose up quickly, and exclaimed in delight: O clever one, thou hast guessed. And she threw round his neck the necklace of her arms, and so chose him as her husband [h]. And she said: See, thy image is reflected a thousand times in these gems that resemble thee; yet look in my eyes, and thou shalt see thyself through them reflected in my heart. Then the King looked into her eyes, and saw himself reflected in them like the sun in a deep lake. And he whispered in the shell of her ear: Thou hast robbed me of myself: give me back myself in thy form. Then the Princess said, in a low voice, looking down: Would'st thou take my sweetness for nothing? What did the bee give the lotus? And the King trembled with passion, and putting his hand beneath her chin, he raised her face and kissed her on her ruby mouth. And in that moment he forgot everything, and he felt his life surging through him like a wave of the sea, and he became blind and deaf, and tottered

[h] This is an allusion to the *swayamwara*, an old ceremony by which a maiden chose her own husband by throwing a garland round his neck.

on his feet. Then Anangarágá roused him from his stupor by saying: Wert thou afraid of losing me? And he said: O my beloved, I am saved from the mouth of death. Then she laughed low, and said: There was no cause for fear. For had I again answered a question to-day, I would have refused to answer to-morrow, even though thou hadst asked me nothing but my own name. But I could scarcely endure to wait till to-morrow, and it is better as it is. Then the King said: And why, O thou rogue, didst thou not refuse to answer before, and save me from torture? And Anangarágá said: It was torture also to me. And yet I know not why, but there was nectar in the poison, and know, O my lord, that this is the nature of women, that they love to torment their lover, and refuse him what they themselves most of all desire.

Then King Súryakánta almost swooned away from excess of joy. And he said: Come, let us leave this place, which is hateful to me as the scene of my sufferings, and let us return without delay to my capital. And the Princess said: As my lord pleases.

Then the King sent Rasakósha, with all the retinue of the Princess, on before. But he himself set out at night alone with his bride. And they rode on slowly, side by side, through the forest in the moonlight, he on a white horse, and she on a black, looking like the beauty of day and night incarnate in mortal form. And at midnight they stopped to rest in the forest. And the King lifted Anangarágá from her horse, and placed her in a bower of creepers under a great tree. And the moon shone with warm rays through the interstices of the leaves as through the marble trellis of a palace terrace. And there on a bed of leaves and flowers, he made her his wife by the Gándharwa[1] marriage rite. And he played with the nooses of her blue-black hair, through which her eyes shone like moonstones in the moonlight; and he wove red *ashóka* flowers in her hair, and hung blue lotuses on her bosom, and put a girdle of white lotuses round her waist, and tied anklets of jasmine blossoms on her feet. And in the ecstasy of his passion, bewildered by her beauty, he exclaimed: Well are thou called Anangarágá, O my beloved; and yet a single name is insufficient to describe the

[1] See *Manu*, III. 26. Though recognised as a legitimate marriage, especially for Kshatriyas, it was simply the union of two lovers without any rites at all. This suits it admirably for fairy tale and romance, and makes it a great favourite with the poets.

infinite variety of thy thousand-rayed loveliness. Thou art Mrigalóchaná, for thine eyes are lustrous and frightened like the antelope's; and Nílanaliní, for thy dark hair is like a pool for the lotuses of thine eyes; and Madanalíláólatá, for those eyes dance with the tremulous light of love; and Shashilékhá, for thou art fair and fragile as a digit of the moon; and Bujalatá, for thy arms are curved and cling like creepers; and Kusumayashtí, for thy body is straight and slender like the stalk of a flower; and Kambukanthí, for thy neck is like a shell; and Rajanícháyá, for the sheen of thy beauty is like that of the night; and Láwanyamúrtí, for thou art the very incarnation of the perfection of loveliness: and Manóhariní, for thou ravishest my soul; and Madalaharí, for thou art a wave of the sea of intoxication; and Alipriyá, for the bees resort to the honey of thy lips, mistaking them for a flower; and Wajrasúchí, for thy intellect is like a diamond needle: and Hémakumbhiní, for thy bosom resembles a pair of golden gourds; and Pulinákritı́, for the curves of thy hips are like the swell of a river bank; and Nánárúpiní, for thy beauty is infinite; and Bhrúkutíchalá, for the play of thy brows is like the lightning in the clouds; and yet all these names are powerless to paint thy celestial and overpowering fascination, which maddens me as I gaze at it. Then Anangarágá said, with a smile : O my lord, thou hast omitted, among all these names, the only one that really belongs to me. And the King said : What is that? Then she said : Thou art my deity, and I am possessed by thee in every particle of my being; and therefore call me Nílírágá, for my devotion[k] to thee shall be constant and indelible as the dye of indigo. And know, O sun of my soul, that without this all the beauty of women is but nectar-poison.

Then the King's heart almost broke in his joy, and he exclaimed : Ha! I have obtained the fruit of my birth. All else is nothingness and futility. What can the future hold for me but this, or its absence, which would be worse than a thousand deaths? And he prayed to the all powerful and self-existent One[l], saying : O Mahéshwara, let this heaven continue for ever, and let the chain of my existence be broken at this point! Or rather, let Time be destroyed for me, and let me remain, beyond its influence, for evermore in this present, this moment of union with my beloved!

[k] *Bhakti* is almost untranslateable. It means the absorbed and total love, faith, devotion of a worshipper for his god.

[l] Shiwa.

And that moon-crested god heard him, and granted his wish. And he shot at that pair of lovers, as they slept in one another's arms in the moonlit creeper bower, a glance of his third eye, and reduced them to ashes. But he said: The chain of their existence cannot yet be broken, for they have not yet earned emancipation by penance and austerities. But they shall meet again, and be husband and wife, in another birth.